THE OUTLAW'S WOMAN

When eighteen-year-old Kelly was brought to trial with the two remaining members of the Bassett gang, the Federal Marshal thought she would be discharged. But ten years imprisonment was the outcome for Kelly. The outlaw leader, Hay Bassett, had not only taught Kelly to use a gun to match his best gunmen, but had also taken her for his woman. Her stepfather, the Bassett gang and now the prison wagon guards had all abused her in one way or another, but Kelly was a born fighter and would escape an unjust fate.

MARK FALCON

THE OUTLAW'S WOMAN

Complete and Unabridged

LINFORD
Leicester

First published in Great Britain in 2003 by
Robert Hale Limited
London

First Linford Edition
published 2004
by arrangement with
Robert Hale Limited
London

British Library CIP Data

Falcon, Mark
    The outlaw's woman.—Large print ed.—
Linford western library
1. Western stories
2. Large type books
I. Title
823.9′14 [F]

ISBN 1–84395–474–5

Published by
F. A. Thorpe (Publishing)
Anstey, Leicestershire

Set by Words & Graphics Ltd.
Anstey, Leicestershire
Printed and bound in Great Britain by
T. J. International Ltd., Padstow, Cornwall

This book is printed on acid-free paper

To Ronald and Phillip Kinsella

1

The group stood silently by the graveside of the outlaw Hay Bassett. It was beside the rock pool in the valley the outlaw had named Paradise — the only paradise he would ever know. The four men looked towards the young girl as the tears splashed down her cheeks.

The outlaw had kept her prisoner with the Bassett gang for over three months, yet in that time it was obvious that he had meant a lot to her. A stranger coming on to the scene would be forgiven for thinking that there were five men by the graveside as the girl was dressed in man's attire — black, low-crowned sombrero, black shirt and pants and black boots. She was slim and could pass herself off as a boy, which she had done to begin with after the man whom she thought had been her father, had cut off her hair and forced her to wear men's clothes. To begin with, the ruse had been of help to her when the Bassett gang arrived at her home after robbing the Mayville bank. The outlaw leader, Hay Bassett, needed help with his injured brother, Cal. When the posse arrived at the house, the girl was amazed to find that her father was intending to join up with the gang and proved his allegiance by shooting the sheriff.

It had seemed such a long time ago since she had been dragged off to join her father, Denver Branch, his two men, Quincey and Hankins and the members of the gang to their hideout in the town of Larkinton. The place was now just a pile of ashes after the law had had a shoot-out with the outlaws and burned the place down.

A lot had happened to the girl since she first arrived in the town with Hay Bassett after she had collapsed with fatigue on the trail. He had stayed with her overnight while the rest of the gang went on ahead. He had not taken advantage of her when he had found out her true sex and had treated her kindly — kindlier than the man she knew as her father in fact.

Kelly took one final look around the beautiful spot and for a few seconds relived her conversations with Jim Tobin, Sandy, Quincey and Hay.

Steve Culley, whom she'd escaped to find again, put his arm around her shoulder and they followed US Marshal Luke Dalton, Joe Lilley and Zeb Boadley back to the horses at the two boulders. They mounted up and Kelly gave a last look at the cabin which had been her home with the outlaw leader. He had said they were on honeymoon in the valley, although he had not married her. But she had been his woman and now part of her was missing — the man who had made her his. She felt confused and could not understand her feelings. She knew she loved Steve Culley, yet she still also loved his father, Hay Bassett.

Once over the narrow ledge they

soon came to the burned-out town. The saloon was the place Kelly wanted Denver Branch to be buried. He had made her life a living hell for over seventeen years and now he could go there himself.

Kelly relived that moment in the valley when Denver Branch had appeared from nowhere and intended killing her for betraying the gang to the law. It had happened so fast. The unarmed Hay Bassett had grabbed Joe Lilley's gun and fired. Steve had thought he was aiming at him and shot back, only to realize that he was not the target, Branch was. Steve had killed his own father, although the man had not recognized him as his son after ten years. Branch was dead and now buried in among the ashes.

They mounted up again. The rest of the posse had gone on ahead with the remnants of the outlaws who had given themselves up. There were only two of the Bassett gang left, Jim Tobin who was wanted by the law for killing his unfaithful wife and her lover besides robbing banks with the Bassett gang, and Hankins, who had been one of Denver Branch's men. Jake Thomas and Ben Harvey had perished in the fire, preferring this to a hanging. Quincey, the other of Branch's men, and Sandy Kaye, whom Kelly had helped on to her horse after his own had been shot from under him after the Hazelworth bank raid, had both been shot by Hay Bassett after they had faced him in a shoot-out back at Kelly's home when she had escaped temporarily from the gang.

For all of her seventeen years Kelly had thought her name had been Kelly Branch, but Denver had put her straight at last before Hay Bassett finally took her as his own. Her real father had been a man called Kelly and Branch had called her that so he would always remember that she was not his own daughter. So in actual fact, her name was Kelly Kelly. This thought brought a slight smile to her face.

She felt Steve's eyes on her as they rode side by side towards Hazelworth and she turned her head and smiled at him. She did not know what life had in store for her now. She could even go to prison for her part in the Hazelworth bank job, but if Steve was prepared to wait for her, she knew she could even survive that. Surely she had survived much worse, for she had already been a prisoner of the Bassett gang for more than three months.

Eventually Hazelworth could be seen in the distance. The rail line and freight terminal were on the edge of town and pens of lowing cattle could be heard as they awaited shipment east.

The townsfolk were expecting them and they were soon lined up on either side of the main street to watch the five ride past.

'Is that the outlaw's woman — the one in black?' Kelly heard a woman ask of her neighbour. 'She's not very old, is she?'

She felt their eyes on her and knew

she would probably be a talking point for several days until they got used to having a woman dressed in man's attire in town.

They all dismounted outside the sheriff's office. Daniel Todd was waiting for them on the boardwalk.

Kelly suddenly felt afraid and looked at the lawman she had been riding with.

'What's going to happen to me, Marshal Dalton?' Kelly asked him as she stood beside her horse.

'I don't know just yet, Kelly. Strictly speaking, you're an outlaw because of the Hazelworth bank job.'

'But she was forced to do it, Luke,' Steve spoke out.

'I reckon the jail's full up anyhow. Hold on a minute and I'll have a word with Sheriff Todd.'

Marshal Dalton went with the sheriff into the latter's office and after a few minutes, Dalton came out.

'If you give me your word you won't skip town, and report to the sheriff daily, maybe you can stay at the hotel or at Mrs Simpson's boarding-house.'

'I'll arrange something, Luke,' Steve told him. He took Kelly's hand. 'We'll put the horses up then I'll find you somewhere to stay.'

Mrs Simpson was not keen on letting out a room to a former outlaw.

'Let's see Miss Dobson before we try the hotel. I know she'd love to meet you. She might even help you out with some women's clothes.'

It was about one o'clock and the restaurant was full. Steve could not see anyone who had taken on his job in his absence and he guessed Sarah Dobson would be too busy to talk just then. He left Kelly at one of the tables while he went into the kitchen.

'I'm back, Miss Dobson,' Steve informed her, as she was ladling stew onto a plate.

'Thank the Lord for that!' she exclaimed, brushing back a lock of dark hair from her perspiring forehead. 'Can you help me out, Steve? I'm fair rushed off my feet.'

Steve hesitated for a fraction of a second and took the plate from her. 'Which table?' he asked.

'Number 3.'

'Right,' Steve nodded. 'I'll talk to you later when the rush is over.'

Kelly was surprised to see Steve delivering the plate to one of the tables nearby. He was obviously used to it.

'I'll bring you something to eat in a minute, Kelly. Miss Dobson's getting a mite flustered in the kichen on her own.'

He was gone again, soon returning with another plate of stew for Kelly.

'Get that down you and you'll feel a heap better I reckon.'

Kelly ate hungrily, but sitting down in a restaurant reminded her of the meals she'd eaten with Hay Bassett. A lump came to her throat as his face flashed into her mind and the thought that she'd never see him again. Maybe it was just as well. He had died as he'd always wanted to — in a shoot-out and not at the end of a rope.

It was soon two o'clock and the restaurant closed until the evening rush. Now was the time to acquaint Kelly with Steve's erstwhile employer.

'This is my girl I told you about, Miss Dobson — Kelly,' he smiled proudly as he presented the slim, boyish-looking girl.

'Waal, I declare!' she exclaimed in amazement.

'We rescued her from Bassett and his gang. I've got to find her somewhere to stay. Mrs Simpson was none too keen on her staying at the boarding-house.'

Sarah Dobson sniffed. 'I don't know what she's got to be so pernickety about — unless she thinks you two are gonna sleep in the same room?'

'I reckon it's because of my appearance,' Kelly smiled. 'I haven't worn women's clothes for over three months now. I almost feel like a boy after all this time — just like my pa — the man I thought was my pa — wanted.'

A quizzical look crossed Sarah Dobson's face. There was obviously much she would like to find out about this strange young woman.

'You can stay with me if you like,' Sarah suggested. 'I've got a spare room upstairs above the restaurant — that's where I live by the way.'

Kelly looked from Sarah to Steve and back again. 'That would be wonderful,' she said huskily and swallowed hard. 'After all that's happened to me lately, it'll feel like somewhere safe — and having another woman around after only men for company will be so . . . so . . . wonderful!' she finished, unable to find another word to describe how she felt.

Sarah Dobson drew her into her womanly bossom and felt the young girl's body shaking with tears that had been held back for so long. 'There, there. You're safe now. Steve and I'll take care of you from now on.'

Kelly helped Sarah Dobson wash and dry the dishes, leaving everywhere spick and span for the evening session.

'What we've got to do now,' said

11

Sarah, 'is to kit you out with some dresses and under garments.'

'I haven't got any money,' Kelly told her.

'I'll tell you what, young woman, if you help out tonight, and every day from now on if you want, you can pay me back with your wages. How's that?'

'I think that would be mighty fine.' Kelly grinned from ear to ear.

2

After being shown her room above the restaurant, Kelly was taken clothes shopping. Steve was dismissed for the afternoon as his presence was definitely not required.

He watched as the two women set off down the main street and was conscious of everyone's eyes on the newcomer to the town. He realized that he had never seen Kelly in a dress before. She had always worn a pair of men's pants more suitable for riding when they met at their usual place by the river which separated the Big B Ranch from the Johnson spread where Steve worked as a ranch hand. He would never forget their first meeting when he and another ranch hand had come upon her bathing naked in the river. The beautiful sight of her would remain in his memory for ever. They had got to know each other better as the weeks went by and their one and only kiss had been abruptly ended by the arrival of Denver Branch and his two henchmen. Branch had left the two men to do their worst with Steve, resulting in some of his ribs being broken as well as other major wounds.

Kelly had not come off unscathed, and Steve still remembered the terrific smack across her face delivered by the enormous bear of a man who passed himself off as her father. That was the last time Steve had seen Kelly for over three months until their eventual meeting in the place called Paradise.

What a brave young woman she had been, Steve marvelled. No one else had escaped from the outlaw hideout of Larkinton before Kelly had managed it under cover of darkness, slipping by the guards up in the rocks by muffling her horse's hoofs.

A warm feeling came over him as he realized she had risked her life just to find him again. How lucky it had been that old Zeb Boadley, returning to Hazelworth after another year of fruitless prospecting, had met her on the trail on her way to Mayville. This town was a few miles away from her old homestead and Steve found out that she had intended looking for him there as well as at his old employer's, Abe Johnson. It was Zeb who had brought the news to Hazelworth and the law, and a mighty important man he had considered himself with such valuable information, for the law had been searching for the outlaws' hideout for many years.

Steve continued with his thoughts over a quiet drink in the saloon, where he could keep an eye out for the return of the women after their shopping expedition.

As they walked down the main street, Kelly looked about her, conscious of the many eyes on her. Through a gap in the buildings she noticed the knoll topped with trees. That was the place she had spent the night with the gang before the bank raid the following morning. Hay's words came back to her as she remembered lying in her bedroll, surrounded by the others. He had been pacing up and down like a caged lion and she could feel the tension inside him. Finally he lay beside her. Their eyes met and he smiled at her, but Kelly had been unable to return the smile and turned her back on him.

She had felt his hand on her shoulder and he called her name quietly.

'Kelly.'

'Yes, Hay?'

She had faced him again and wondered what was on his mind.

'When we go into that bank tomorrow, I want you to do as you're told. You, Hankins, Quincey and your pa will fill the bags with the money, while the rest of us hold guns on the cashiers. When I say 'out' I want you to get on your horse and ride. It's every man for himself. Do you understand? And wear a neckerchief over your face until you get out of sight.'

Kelly had protested once again that she would be hopeless as a bank robber and pleaded to be left out of it. He had smiled and patted her on the arm. 'You'll be OK,' was his promise.

'Kelly, why have you stopped? The dress shop is just ahead. What's so interesting up on that hill?'

Kelly was brought back to the present day by Sarah Dobson's voice beside her.

'I was remembering the night before the bank raid. We spent it on that knoll among the trees. I didn't want to take part, but if I hadn't, I would either have been shot by my so-called pa, or Hay Bassett. If I helped do the bank job then that meant I would be as guilty as the rest of them so that I wouldn't betray them to the law.' Kelly sighed deeply. 'I betrayed them anyway.' She looked into Sarah Dobson's frank, open face. The woman's mouth was slightly open in amazement at what she was hearing.

'Come on, girl, let's get you fitted out

like a woman once more. Then maybe you'll forget all about it and start living again.'

Kelly smiled at her. 'Thanks. It might help . . . but I doubt it.'

Deep in her heart, Sarah Dobson doubted it too.

When the two women emerged from the shop, Kelly was unrecognizable from the 'boy' who had gone inside. It felt strange to Kelly after all that time to look and feel like a woman again. Would Steve approve of her new appearance? she wondered. She was sure he would. Hay had promised to buy her a dress and there came a quick stab to her heart as she remembered how the posse had come upon them before he was able to carry out his promise. How she wished she could get the outlaw completely out of her mind. How long would it take? she wondered — if at all.

'I've got to report to the sheriff every day as one of the conditions of staying out of a jail cell,' Kelly remembered.

'Do you want me to come in with you?' Sarah asked with concern.

Kelly thought about it for a moment. 'Would you?'

'Of course. I can vouch for your good behaviour,' she smiled.

Sheriff Daniel Todd looked up from his desk and it was obvious that he was pleased to see two women as opposed to men enter his domain.

'What can I do for you ladies?' he asked brightly.

'I'm just letting you know I'm still around, Sheriff,' said Kelly.

He looked at her for a moment, then it dawned on him who the young woman was — the outlaw Hay Bassett's woman.

'Surprising the difference clothes can make. No one would believe you could rob a bank, dressed like that.'

'I didn't want to, Sheriff, believe me.'

'Young Andy Cole paid the price for you and the Bassett gang's visit — he paid with his life,' the sheriff said tersely.

19

'If I could have stopped it, I would have,' said Kelly quietly.

'Maybe so or maybe not. In any case, a good man died that day.'

'Any idea when the trial date will be set?' Kelly asked him.

'The circuit judge will arrive next month. You'll have to stand trial with the other two members of the gang who survived the shoot-out and fire in Larkinton.'

'Can you give me any idea how I stand, Sheriff? It wasn't my idea to be an outlaw. I was their prisoner. I escaped from them once, only to be captured again. All I wanted to do was be a woman and live with Steve Culley,' she explained.

'Even Culley turned out to be Hay Bassett's son!' the sheriff hissed.

'It was Steve Culley who killed his father. Didn't Marshal Dalton explain this to you, Sheriff?'

'Sure. He also told me that Hay Bassett saved your life 'cos your pa, who turned out not to be your pa, was about to shoot you. Sounds as if you got pretty pally with Hay Bassett. He even took you for his woman!'

Kelly could not deny it. Neither could she deny helping Sandy Kaye, enabling him to make a getaway. It wouldn't matter what she said to this lawman, obviously he was not in the mood to take her side in the matter.

'It's a wonder you don't want to visit your friends in the cells — Tobin and Hankins.'

'They're not my friends. Hankins was one of Branch's men who helped another, Quincey, to beat Steve half to death, so I've no feelings for him. Jim Tobin wasn't too bad towards me after I'd proved myself.'

'And what might that mean?' Todd frowned.

'Denver Branch intended joining up with the Bassett gang but I didn't know that. When Hay's brother was shot in the Mayville bank job I came across them by the river and they made me take them back to our place to see to him. To prove to Hay that he would be loyal, Denver shot the Mayville sheriff. The gang thought I was a boy because Denver had already cut my hair and made me dress like one. I kept up this pretence until Sandy Kaye staged a fist fight with me and knocked me unconscious. But Sandy Kaye didn't get off lightly. I gave almost as good as I got and the gang respected me after that, but it was then that my true sex was revealed. Hay Bassett had already gone on ahead to Paradise and he was angry when he saw how I'd been treated by his men. He was kind to me and didn't touch me until I escaped from them. After he'd caught up with me again and brought me back to Larkinton, and Paradise, he . . . he took me . . . as his woman,' Kelly finished quietly and hung her head.

Sheriff Todd stood up and put his hands on Kelly's shoulders. 'I'm sorry, young lady. If there's any justice you'll get off lightly or altogether. It'll be up to the judge, but I'll speak up for you.'

'I appreciate that, Sheriff.' Kelly looked at Sarah Dobson, standing quietly all this time, and wondered if she'd still stand by her after all she'd just heard.

'I'm taking care of her, Sheriff,' Sarah told the lawman. 'She'll be working for me in the restaurant until the trial.'

'That's good of you, ma'am.' He turned again to Kelly. 'Drop by every day, miss — just so's I know you're still around.'

Kelly nodded and both women left the lawman's office.

3

The circuit judge arrived in Hazelworth four weeks later, but Kelly and the other two members of the Bassett gang were not to get their turn to be tried until after the outlaws who had holed-up in Larkinton, and were not members of Hay Bassett's gang, had been tried first. They were given various sentences of between ten years to life imprisonment, or death by hanging. Kelly, Tobin and Hankins were to be tried three weeks after this.

The weeks before the trial were the happiest Kelly had spent in her whole life. She enjoyed working in the restaurant with Steve and Sarah Dobson. She was well fed and the room she was given to sleep in was comfortable. When not in Steve's company, she spent her time with Sarah Dobson and it was almost like having a mother again. She had never known her real mother, but Jean, whom Denver Branch had married when her real mother had died giving birth to her, had been as good.

Denver Branch had hated Kelly since her birth, not only because it had caused her mother's death, but because she had been another man's child. She had learned these new facts when the gang had caught up with her again at the homestead after she had escaped from them. Branch also hated her because Kelly was seeing Steve Culley by the river when Jean had gone into labour with Branch's son. Both Jean and the baby had died, in spite of Kelly's efforts. Jean had been over forty when she conceived and the doctor, when he arrived too late, explained to Branch that it was not Kelly's fault. Despite this, Denver Branch still blamed Kelly and partly for revenge had cut off her hair and made her become his 'son'.

Lawyers were few and far between

and the last of the Bassett gang had to make do with the US marshal for any support. Hankins was given thirty years and Tobin was sentenced to death by hanging. This came as no surprise to Jim Tobin as he expected nothing less.

Kelly was surprised to find herself feeling sorry for the man and although he had professed to hate all women because of the experience he had had with his unfaithful wife, Jim Tobin had found himself respecting the young girl who had lived among them for three months. Kelly recalled how he had carried the buckets of water for her from the stream after she was recovering from her beating at the hands of Sandy Kaye. In return she had washed the man's shirts for him.

Tobin and Hankins told the judge that Kelly was forced to belong to the gang and that she had betrayed them to the law. This went in her favour.

It was now Kelly's turn to be judged. The court was held in the saloon and no alcohol was allowed to be served while the court was in session.

'State your name,' the judge told Kelly.

'Kelly, sir,' she replied.

'And your surname?'

'Kelly,' she replied.

'Don't try being funny with me, young woman. Tell us your name.'

'Kelly Kelly,' she replied seriously.

'I'll have you for contempt of court before I even try you for the other offences!' The judge's voice rose in annoyance.

'My real father's surname was Kelly, sir. My stepfather called me Kelly so he wouldn't forget that I wasn't his, so my name is Kelly Kelly, sir.'

The judge sighed and continued with the trial.

Besides Tobin and Hankins' testimony that Kelly was a reluctant outlaw, others spoke up for her, Steve Culley, Marshal Dalton, Sheriff Todd and Sarah Dobson. All looked well for Kelly until another witness was called: the bystander, by the name of John Worth, who had shot Sandy Kaye's horse from under him. He was asked what had happened on the day of the bank raid. He told the court that he had fired towards one of the gang and missed, but hit his horse instead. The bank robber who had sandy-coloured hair was picked up by what he thought was a boy with red hair and the two rode off on the boy's horse.

'Is that 'boy' in the court?' the judge asked him.

'Yes, Your Honour, it's that young woman standing in the dock.'

The members of the court laughed at this.

'So this young woman in the dock is in fact the boy you saw escape with the other bank robber on the back of his horse?'

'That's right, Your Honour,' was his self-satisfied reply.

'Was this boy masked at all?' asked the judge.

'Yes he was, Your Honour.'

'Then how can you positively identify

the prisoner in the dock as this masked boy?'

The man's face dropped slightly at this. 'Well, she's got the same colour hair and she came into town with the law, didn't she?'

'Miss Kelly,' the judge began, 'you don't deny belonging to the Bassett gang, do you?'

'No, Your Honour, sir,' replied Kelly.

'And were you the outlaw who assisted the sandyhaired bank robber to escape on the back of your horse?'

Kelly hesitated at his question, but nodded. 'I helped Sandy Kaye get on to my horse,' she admitted.

'Was that the same man who beat you badly when you first arrived in Larkinton?'

'Yes, it was,' Kelly replied.

'Then if, as you say, you were forced to do the Hazelworth bank job, why didn't you just leave him, or go to the law and give yourself up? The other members of the gang had gone on without you,' the judge pointed out.

'They said that the law wouldn't believe me.'

'And by your actions in saving one of the gang members, did you think that would help you make anyone believe you?'

Kelly shrugged her shoulders and looked down. 'I just did it on instinct. I didn't think it over.'

'Which one of the gang shot the cashier in the bank?' the judge asked.

'I didn't actually see him do it, but Jake Thomas was the last one out after I heard a shot fired inside the bank. Hay Bassett was angry at this 'cos he didn't like unnecessary killing.'

'And where is Jake Thomas now?' was the judge's next question.

'He was one of gang who died in the shoot-out, or fire, in Larkinton, sir.'

'So we can't try this man for killing the bank cashier,' the judge shook his head and sighed. 'We've only got your word for it that this Jake Thomas did the actual shooting.'

'I don't tell lies, Your Honour.'

'You were brought up by an outlaw, you lived among outlaws — you even became an outlaw leader's woman, I've been informed. And do you expect this court to believe a word you say?'

Kelly's hazel eyes flashed. 'All what you say is true — sir — but that don't make me a liar. I escaped the gang and they caught me again. Robbing banks and living with outlaws was the last thing I ever wanted to do! I even got word to the law when I escaped and told them where the hideout was. If I'd enjoyed my life with those men I wouldn't have betrayed them, would I?' Kelly flung back at him.

This was the Kelly, Hankins and Jim Tobin had grown to know. The fire had returned in her.

'How old are you, Miss Kelly?' the judge asked.

Kelly looked surprised. She thought he would have known this already.

'I'm seventeen, sir.'

'And when will you be eighteen?'

Kelly thought for a moment. She had

31

lost all track of the date or month.

'In June, sir,' she said at last.

'We're in July now, so were you eighteen last month or next year?'

'I must be eighteen then,' said Kelly.

'It seems you can't even tell the truth about your age, young woman,' the man scoffed.

'I don't carry a calendar around with me,' Kelly snapped.

The people in the court laughed at this, which did not please the judge. He could not stand anyone talking back at him as it undermined his authority.

'The jury will now consider their verdict — whether or not you were a member of the Bassett gang.'

US Marshal Luke Dalton jumped to his feet. 'Hold on there, Judge. This can't be right. The jury can't give any other verdict than that Kelly did belong to the gang. She was forced into it so this must make a difference.'

'There's no difference at all, Marshal Dalton. She either belonged to the gang, or she didn't. There's nothing else to consider. Court adjourned. The jury will bring in their verdict at two o'clock this afternoon.'

The judge swept out leaving the court with open mouths. Kelly was returned to the jail pending the result of the jury's decision. Other than Tobin and Hankins, the criminals brought in from Larkinton had now been dispatched to jail in the next county which was big enough to hold them all, and also had the facilities for hangings. There was now room for Kelly.

It would be two hours before the verdict was reached, and there could be only one outcome — guilty.

4

Steve and Sarah hurried back to the restaurant for the lunch-time rush. There were more people in town than usual to hear the Bassett gang trial and the restaurant did a roaring trade. Sarah and Steve, however, would have preferred not to have to work at all as their hearts were not in it. Both had the deep-seated feeling that things had not gone well for Kelly after the judge's summing-up. He had given the jury a one-verdict outcome. Everyone knew it was unfair and the two in particular hoped that there would be clemency granted. They had not been allowed to talk to Kelly before the verdict was announced at two o'clock and knew what a state Kelly must be in at that moment.

The restaurant closed earlier than usual so they could get back to the saloon court by two.

There was hubbub as everyone waited expectantly for the show to begin. Kelly meant nothing to most of them and it was all good entertainment.

Kelly was led to her seat at the side of the bar by Sheriff Todd. She looked at the man and noticed the pity in his eyes. He was obviously aware of the outcome of the verdict in advance — as was everyone.

'All rise!' came the call, as Judge Dean swept in and sat down on a high seat behind the bar, surrounded by bottles of whiskey. The people took this as permission to seat themselves.

'Members of the jury, have you reached your verdict?' he asked the twelve assorted men from the town.

'We have, Your Honour,' said the foreman of the jury, 'but we would like to express our concern at the way the charge was put. The young woman was obviously forced to join up with the gang as her stepfather made her come with him and his two men. We feel she deserves clemency because of the way she informed the law of the Bassett hideout, also on account of her young age, and also because she's a girl.'

'Your remarks have been noted,' said the judge. 'What is your verdict, guilty of belonging to the Bassett gang, or not guilty?'

'The question is impossible to answer, Your Honour.'

'There has to be an answer. Did she ride with the Bassett gang and rob the Hazelworth bank? They are simple enough questions.'

'Well, yes, she did that, Your Honour.'

'Then the verdict is guilty!' the judge snapped.

'Yes, but . . . '

'No buts. Because of her age and sex, and as there is some doubt that she wanted to belong to the gang, I will take these mitigating circumstances into consideration. Instead of giving her thirty years' imprisonment, I'll give her ten.' He turned towards Kelly. 'And you can think yourself lucky, young woman, that I didn't give you the full term.'

Kelly didn't feel lucky at all. She knew she didn't deserve to spend any time in jail. Her heart sank and she looked across at Steve and Sarah.

'That's not right!' Steve stood up and shouted. 'She should be set free immediately.'

'Sit down!' Judge Dean commanded. 'I'll increase the sentence at the next outburst.'

Steve could see the tears welling up into Kelly's eyes and he desperately wanted to hold and comfort her and to take her away from the place so they could be together again. He felt so useless. He wondered what Hay Bassett would have done in the circumstances. No doubt he would have grabbed a gun from someone and held up the court with it and led Kelly to safety. He knew the man had loved her enough for this as he had given his life to save hers. Yet here Steve stood, doing nothing at all. He felt ashamed of himself. Maybe his father, Hay

Bassett, had been twice the man he was?

Kelly hung her head as she was led away to the jail. She did not want anyone to see the tears. She had received many a blow from Denver Branch over the years and had never cried and she did not intend doing so now. But ten years . . . She would be twenty-eight by the time her sentence ended. No man would wait that long for her. She knew it was best not to think about Steve any more and let him get on with his life without her.

Luke Dalton came across to Steve and Sarah Dobson and looked slightly ashamed at the outcome. He had been certain that Kelly would have got off. If only she hadn't helped Sandy Kaye on to the back of her horse after the bank robbery then perhaps the judge would have thought differently and let her go free?

'Can we appeal, Marshal?' Steve asked the tall man.

'We could try, but I don't hold out

much hope of a reversal of the verdict. Kelly's young, she'll still be young when she comes out. I don't suppose you can wait that long for her?' the lawman asked.

'I can't just abandon her — not after all she's been through,' he replied quietly.

'There's nothing you can do about it, Steve,' the lawman told him. 'After ten years both of you will have changed. It's not as if you've been together long; you hardly know each other really.'

'I know enough about her to know that I'll never get her out of my mind, no matter how long we're apart. I guess my father knew her longer than I did — and better,' he finished, a little bitterly.

Dalton touched the younger man on the arm in sympathy.

'Will I be able to see her before they take her off to prison?' Steve asked.

'I'll see to it. Come with me. You can come too, Sarah, if you want?'

The buxom woman nodded, tears not too far away from her eyes either, and the three of them walked out of the saloon and down the street to the sheriff's office.

'Some visitors to see Kelly,' Luke said to Todd, as they entered the office.

'Sure,' the man nodded, and his voice betrayed his feelings. He, too, expected Kelly to get off, or at least get a shorter or suspended sentence. He led the way through to the cells at the back of his office.

'Kelly!' Steve rushed forward. 'Oh Kelly, I'm so sorry!'

'It's a crying shame, and it should never be allowed to happen!' Sarah Dobson exclaimed.

Kelly sat with her hands loosely in her lap on the bunk, her face pale and emotionless. At last she stood up and walked slowly towards them. Her small hands gripped the bars of the cell and Steve noticed them trembling slightly.

She looked at Sarah Dobson first. 'I want to thank you, Miss Dobson, for all your kindness to me. I won't ever forget it. I'm sorry I won't be able to work for you any more. These last weeks have been the happiest of my whole life.'

Her eyes went to Steve's, and for a brief second she saw Hay Bassett standing there before her.

'I'm glad you found me again, Steve. I'll never forget you — but promise me you'll forget all about me. I want you to get on with your life — find someone else — get married and have children. I want you to be happy. Don't worry about me, I'll be just fine,' she tried her hardest to assure him.

'I'll get a job near the prison and visit you as often as they'll allow,' he said earnestly.

She touched his hand through the bars and shook her head.

'No. Don't prolong it. Put me out of your mind — please . . . Promise me. It's what I want.'

He shook his head. 'No. I can't promise that.'

'You must. It's over between us. Get on with your life. Goodbye, my love.'

She turned from them and returned

41

to the bunk and sat down. Her face became expressionless again and it was as if she had returned in her mind to another life away from this one.

Luke Dalton and Daniel Todd had hovered in the background. Both were tough, hard lawmen, but even they felt their throats turn dry and had difficulty in swallowing.

Sarah Dobson, the kind, motherly woman who had become such a friend to Steve and Kelly over the past weeks, put her arm around the young man as they left the cells. Steve turned once more to take another look at the woman he'd always love, but it was as if he had never been there. He had lost her again.

Sarah Dobson had another thing on her mind. Kelly had been vomiting in the mornings before she stood for trial. It could have been through worry and tension, but she had a feeling it was due to something else entirely — that Kelly was now carrying Hay Bassett's baby. Inwardly she prayed that she was mistaken.

5

Early the next morning the prison wagon arrived outside the sheriff's office. The early hour was to prevent a large crowd forming to watch the three members of the Bassett gang leave town for their journey to the next county.

Steve Culley and Sarah Dobson knew of the time the wagon would leave and were waiting outside on the boardwalk. Steve had considered not watching the girl he loved leave him for ever as it might have upset Kelly. He knew he would be more than upset himself. It was still on his mind to try and rescue her before she left but he knew this would be a stupid idea. A lot of people could get hurt. The idea had not entirely left him though.

One of the two guards jumped down from his seat on the wagon and went inside the office. A moment or two later, Hankins, Tobin and then Kelly came out. Steve moved forward and touched her arm. Her feet were manacled and her wrists were hand-cuffed in front of her. The guard jabbed Steve in the ribs with the butt of his rifle and pushed him out of the way. Kelly glanced at him briefly but was pushed forward towards the back of the wagon and climbed up the two steps to reach the inside.

There was a wooden form along both lengths of the wagon with enough room for the occupants' feet in the centre. A chain was being put around Hankins' and Tobin's waist and attached to a metal bar behind them. Kelly then had this indignity inflicted upon her. Any thought of escape before they reached their destination was out of the question.

It was quite dark inside the wagon, with only a small opening with two bars down it as the only source of light. The two guards could peer in if they wanted to, just to make sure the prisoners were not attempting anything.

Sheriff Todd signed his name to a form and now everything was official for the transportation of the three prisoners.

The wagon was soon off, the two horses urged into a trot.

Steve accompanied Sarah Dobson back to the restaurant. He put his arm around the woman's shaking shoulders as they walked along the street in an attempt to comfort her, but he was unable to comfort himself.

The two sat together and drank coffee, each mouthful almost choking them.

'She didn't look at all well, did she, Sarah?' he said quietly.

'I reckon I know why,' she replied.

He looked at her sharply. 'What do you know?' he asked. She hesitated, wondering whether she ought to voice her fears in case she was wrong.

'I caught her vomiting in the morning two or three times lately.'

They looked at each other and Sarah

wondered if Steve had guessed what she had been intimating.

'She's expecting Hay Bassett's child?' he asked.

'I can't be sure of course, but she had all the signs.'

'That clinches it!' Steve exclaimed, getting up from his seat. 'No way can she go to prison for ten years and bear a child inside. The baby'll be my half-brother or sister,' it dawned on him.

Sarah could see his mind working.

'You're not considering doing something foolish, are you, Steve?'

He flashed her a look.

'I've gotta do something. I'm afraid I'm gonna have to leave you in the lurch again, Sarah. I think mebbe this is the last time I'll be seeing you.'

'There's nothing I can say or do to stop you?' she asked half-heartedly, but she knew his mind was made up.

'Afraid not. I won't get much of a head start and I'll be missed at lunch-time. Luke Dalton'll guess where

I've gone straight away no doubt.'

'You realize that if you help Kelly escape then you'll be a wanted man, too?'

The young man nodded. 'Just like my father was. Like father like son, eh?'

'There's a vast amount of difference between you. The only thing you've got in common is that you both love and loved Kelly.'

He nodded. 'That's a fact.'

Steve came and stood at the back of Sarah's chair and put his hands on the woman's shoulders.

'Sorry to run out on you again, Sarah. You've bin mighty good to me — and Kelly. I won't forget it.'

She turned to face him and smiled slightly. 'I'll try and stall the marshal for a while somehow. That'll give you a bit more time. But don't go killing anyone if you can help it. You don't want to be a killer like your father was.'

'I'll try not to. But I'm getting Kelly back whatever happens,' he vowed.

★ ★ ★

Jim Tobin and Hankins had not, as yet, had a chance to speak to Kelly. They had stood side by side in the dock at their trial, but it was impossible to converse.

'I'm sorry you're in this mess, Kelly,' Tobin told her.

'If she hadn't betrayed us to the law, she wouldn't be here now,' Hankins pointed out.

'Why did you?' Tobin asked. 'I thought you and Hay were on pretty good terms. In fact I thought mebbe you were in love with him.'

'I probably was,' she agreed. 'But after the bank job I knew I couldn't go on like that. He'd never touched me until he came looking for Sandy and me. As you know, he left Sandy to walk back to Larkinton, although he did send someone to fetch him. Hay tried having me, but I fought him off.'

'The scratches on his face,' Hankins put in.

'Yes. He left me alone when he knew I didn't want it, but I could no longer trust him. Before, I had always looked to him to protect me from the rest of you. Besides which, it was a rotten life for me, living with all you men.'

Tobin nodded. He could forgive her for betraying them all now. Hankins, on the other hand had no such feelings.

The prison wagon had by now travelled the road for two hours. Kelly's insides were heaving and her two companions could see she was in trouble.

'Guard, the lady's sick!' Jim Tobin shouted out.

'Shut up in there! We'll stop in another hour,' came the reply.

'Have a heart!' Tobin called out again. 'She's gonna throw up any second.'

The guards exchanged glances and considered whether this was just some ploy to escape.

'Hurry it up!' Tobin yelled.

The horses were pulled to a stop and

the wheel brake applied. Both guards jumped down and one rolled himself a smoke while the other unlocked the door and looked in. It was obvious that Tobin was telling the truth that Kelly was indeed feeling ill. He unlocked the chain round her waist and pulled her forward, helping her to alight from the wagon.

He had come none to soon and Kelly was soon heaving her insides out.

The guard looked away in disgust.

'I need to go to the privy,' Kelly told him.

'Go at the side of the wagon,' he grunted.

'I want some privacy. It's my right,' she said.

'OK, but make it quick. Go behind that rock over there,' he pointed about ten yards away.

'I shall need my hands free. It's easier for a man,' she pointed out.

He thought for a minute as he considered whether she might try to escape. But where to? She wouldn't get far in those leg hobbles. He waved his arm for her to go.

The two guards talked together outside the wagon. 'She's quite a looker,' said the guard who had just released Kelly. 'Yeah, I wouldn't mind a bit,' the other grinned.

'She'll probably enjoy it,' the other laughed. 'Give me five minutes with her and then you can have your turn.'

The guard moved off towards the rock and some enjoyment.

Kelly had just finished rearranging her clothes when the guard appeared.

'I might as well check that you ain't concealing any weapons in them petticoats,' he grinned.

The man reminded her of Quincey and she could tell he had the same thoughts in his mind.

Although she had felt numb as she entered the wagon in Hazelworth, one thing had implanted itself in her brain: the guard who had shackled her was the same one who came towards her now, and he wore his gun on his left side. In spite of everything, Kelly was quick to realize this would be an advantage — for her.

He came up to her and looked down at her pretty young face. 'Shall we begin the investigation, Missy?'

Surprisingly, Kelly smiled up at him. 'You're a fine-looking man, mister. It's a pity I'm going where I'm going. We could perhaps get more — er — closer.'

His eyebrow arched at her sudden friendliness. She was still smiling at him and he pulled her towards him. He felt her left hand caressing his face, and it felt good. What he did not feel, however, was his gun being drawn slowly from its holster with her right hand.

'You were that outlaw's woman, weren't you?' he asked.

'I was,' Kelly answered.

'Then you'll know what's what. Get yourself down on the ground and spread your legs. I'm gonna enjoy looking for any concealed weapons on yer.'

'The only weapon I've got on me, Mr Guard sir — is yours!'

The sound of the click as the hammer was pulled back made him draw in his breath. The last thing he heard was an explosion.

The man fell to the ground, his eyes wide in astonishment. Kelly knew the gunshot would bring the other guard and she quickly lay beside the man, pulling him on to her. She shut her eyes, pretending that it was she who had been shot.

'Bill!' he half questioned. 'What did you go and kill her for — afore I'd had my turn at her?'

Kelly pulled back the hammer again.

As she fired point blank at the man she said, 'No, Mr Guard, it was me who shot him.'

The second guard lay beside the first. Kelly got to her feet and looked down at the two men who had both had the same intentions towards her.

Now what? she wondered. Find the keys to the shackles of course! And then? Kelly shrugged her shoulders. What would Hay do next? she wondered, as she walked towards the prison wagon, keys that she had taken from the first guard's body jingling in her fingers.

6

When Kelly reached the prison wagon her whole body was shaking and her arms and legs felt weak. She just managed to unlock the wagon door and open it and climb up the two steps to her two companions.

'Hell, Kelly, what on earth's been going on?'

'I should think that's obvious,' Hankins said, indicating the gun in Kelly's hand with a jerk of his head. The men had heard two shots from the direction of the rock but could not see anything as they were chained to the bench and the small, barred opening faced a different direction.

'You killed them both?' Jim Tobin wanted confirmation.

She was still shaking and sat down opposite to them.

'I know I did it — but it was as if

someone else had done it — that someone else had taken over my body.'

'I'll have to try that excuse if ever the occasion comes up,' Hankins grinned.

'Was it necessary to kill them both?' Jim asked her quietly.

'That, coming from you!' Hankins inserted.

'No man touches me unless I give him permission,' Kelly said firmly. 'If they hadn't tried to rape me I would have served my time without another word.'

'Remind me to ask your permission if I ever want to — '

'That will never happen, Hankins! Especially not from you!' Kelly hissed.

'You've got three notches on your gun now, you've killed one more than me,' Jim informed her.

'Yeah, she killed that feller in Mayville, didn't she? Doing a young girl a favour, weren't it?' said Hankins.

'Who were you doing a favour for this time?' Jim laughed.

A small smile crossed Kelly's lips.

'Myself and you two, I guess. The remnants of the Bassett gang.'

She began to unlock the chains from their legs, arms and waist. 'They wanted to make me sheriff in Mayville for doing what I've just done to the guards. I can't see no difference myself.'

'What'll we do now?' Jim asked her, as if she had taken command. 'There are two horses and three of us.'

Kelly had by now stopped shaking and her mind began to work clearly again.

'You'll have to wear the guards' uniforms and drive the wagon for as far as possible until we can get another horse.' She looked from one man to the other. 'We'd better get a move on as someone might come along.'

The two men did her bidding without hesitation or argument. It was as if she had taken over from Hay Bassett as the outlaw leader.

They donned the uniforms at the spot the two guards were killed. They both looked very different in the blue jackets edged with yellow and the black peaked caps. It was a well-known fact that people only saw the uniform and hardly gave the person inside it another look. They could pass themselves off as guards quite easily.

They carried the two guards to the prison wagon and sat them on the benches.

'Did we oughta chain them up?' Hankins asked Kelly.

'They might look more like prisoners, I guess,' she said quietly. She could hardly believe what she was saying and what she had just done.

'C'mon, let's get going,' Jim Tobin urged.

'Before we go, is there a drink up there?' she asked the men, as they climbed aboard behind the horses.

Tobin handed her down a canteen and took a drink himself out of the other one.

Kelly got in the back of the wagon with the two dead guards. She felt in their pockets to see if they had any money in them. They would need money to buy food and another horse — unless of course they stole one. She didn't like that idea, but if it had to be done, then it had to, and unless they rode bare-back, they would need saddles and tack.

The wagon moved off again, a little faster than it had done before.

By noon they had reached the outskirts of a town and they pulled off of the road and hid the wagon among some trees.

'Jim, unhitch the horses and ride one of them into town. I've got twenty dollars here that I found in the guards' pockets. It won't go far, but you can either buy a horse with it, or steal one and buy three saddles.'

'Have you forgotten the weight of three saddles, Kelly?' Tobin reminded her. 'Let Hankins come too and then each horse can have a saddle on its back.'

'And what's to prevent him from keeping on riding?' she said. 'Sorry,

Hankins, but I don't trust you — never have — and especially not since you beat Steve near to death.'

'And do you trust me, Kelly?' Tobin asked her.

'I'll have to, won't I?' She eyed him levelly.

'Don't worry, you can depend on me — unless of course something happens to prevent me coming back for you. I think mebbe we'd better leave these coats and hats behind or it'll bring attention to ourselves.'

Kelly nodded in agreement.

Hankins and Tobin now wore the guards' guns on their hips and as Kelly looked up at them in the saddle, it seemed as if they had gone back in time and that nothing had happened in between.

She waved them off and sat back and waited.

It was around four in the afternoon when they finally returned to her. Jim Tobin led a black mare and Kelly remembered her own mare left back in

Hazelworth. She was sorry she hadn't got it now and wondered who would be its new owner. The mare was saddled and Kelly noticed the two riders' horses also had saddles on their backs.

'Did you beg, borrow or steal that lot?' Kelly asked the men.

'A bit of all three,' Jim smiled. He looked quite good-looking when he smiled, Kelly observed. She hadn't noticed it before. She wondered about his age. He looked about forty she guessed, but it was hard to tell.

'What are we gonna do with the wagon?' Hankins asked her.

'There was a ravine back there a mile,' said Kelly. 'I reckon we'd better push it over the edge. But first of all we must do something about their faces.'

'What's that?' Hankins asked with a frown.

'You'll see. Undress the smallest guard and throw the shirt and pants over here,' said Kelly.

As the men began pulling off the dead man's shirt and pants, Kelly began to take off her dress.

Jim Tobin turned and his mouth opened wide. Kelly was soon dressing herself in the guard's clothes.

'Going back to being a boy again, Kelly?' Jim grinned. 'Shame. You look good in a dress.'

She allowed a small smile to cross her lips. 'Thanks,' she said, 'but it's easier riding in men's pants. The only thing missing is my gun,' she announced. 'I feel quite naked without it.'

'We'll get you one later on,' Jim told her. 'Now come on, let's get this over with.'

Tobin and Hankins donned the guards' jackets and peaked caps while they rode the wagon. When they reached the edge of the ravine Kelly called them to stop.

'Before we go any further, put my dress on that one.' She pointed to the first guard whose clothes she was now wearing. 'He was interested in investigating my petticoats, so he can wear them now. If ever the bodies are found, by then they'll be so decomposed that they won't be recognizable. But they might think this one is me, dressed in my clothes. Is there any axle grease around?' she asked.

'What's up your sleeve now, girl?' Hankins frowned, and looked around for a grease pot. 'Found some!' he announced.

'Have we got any matches?' she asked.

Jim looked in the pocket of the jacket he was wearing. 'There's some here. Are you gonna set light to the wagon?'

'No, but first we'll pour some grease over their faces.' Kelly tore two strips from her petticoat and placed a strip on each face. She smeared more grease over them and set them alight. She turned away as the flames burned through the material and only turned back when the flames had died down.

'What do they look like?' she asked, not wanting to see the charred faces she had made unrecognizable.

'I doubt if anyone would know them

now,' said Jim. 'You're a devious one and no mistake. You're like two different women.'

'I wonder where I learned it all from, Jim?' She smiled slightly.

'What do we do with the guards' uniforms?' Hankins wanted to know.

'We'll burn them,' said Kelly. 'We don't want any evidence lying around.'

Tobin poured some of the grease on to the uniforms and set light to them. When the flames had died down Tobin said with some urgency in his voice, 'Come on, let's get rid of this wagon.'

All three pushed the wagon to the edge and with another quick shove, over the top it went, bouncing from rock to rock in its descent to become a mass of matchwood.

7

Steve Culley knew that the prison wagon had two hours' start on him, but he was surprised that he had not come across it yet. He had ridden at a fair pace and knew that the prison wagon would not have gone faster than a horse and rider.

He reached a town and decided to look around to see if the wagon had made a scheduled stop. The office of the local lawman would be the best bet, he reckoned, but he had no intention of asking about the wagon from that quarter.

On the boardwalk outside the town marshal's office sat an old man smoking a briar pipe.

'Afternoon,' Steve said civilly.

The old codger grinned at him toothlessly.

'Could you tell me if the prison

wagon from Hazelworth has stopped here?'

'Nope,' came the reply.

'Does it usually stop here?' Steve asked.

'Yep,' came the monosyllabic reply.

'Would it have bypassed the town for once, do you reckon?'

'Nope,' the old man answered. It occurred to Steve that the old fellow was unable to say anything else.

Steve was at a loss to know what to do next. He had not passed the wagon on his way to Clark County prison, so where on earth could it be now? He was feeling a mite worried.

'How far is Clark County?' Steve asked him, hoping he knew more words than just 'yep' and 'nope'.

'Four hours' ride,' he replied, for which Steve was grateful.

Steve touched his hat to the old man in thanks and turned his horse's head around to continue his search for the wagon. As he rode, he had an uneasy feeling in his gut. He was sure something was wrong.

'Well, boys,' said Kelly as the three arrived at a cross-roads, 'I reckon this is the parting of the ways. We'll be less likely to be caught if we're on our own. When the law eventually realizes that the wagon isn't gonna arrive at the prison, they'll be looking for the three of us.'

'I'd rather we stuck together,' was Hankins' opinion.

Kelly snorted with derision. 'I bet you would! I don't reckon you've ridden alone for the whole of your life. You've always got to have back-up — like Quincey for instance. You are only satisfied when you're doing someone else's bidding.'

'I'd rather we stuck together, Kelly,' Jim Tobin said, as the three sat their horses at the crossroads. 'I've a feeling you're gonna need some help soon — in about seven months' time?' He watched her eyes for confirmation of his guess.

She lowered her eyes for a moment and was silent.

'I am right, ain't I?' Jim enquired.

'What you gettin' at, Jim?' Hankins wanted to know.

'That I'm expecting Hay's baby,' Kelly announced, looking at the men in turn.

'Hell!' Hankins exclaimed. 'I mebbe shouldn't say this, Kelly, but it's done us a favour, you being nauseous and all, made the guards unshackle you for a while.'

Both Kelly and Tobin gave the man a look of disgust.

At that moment the three heard the sound of horses' hoofs from the direction they had come. It was a stagecoach heading towards them.

'We'll need some money,' Hankins reminded them. 'Shall we have a go?'

'We haven't got masks,' Jim reminded him.

'No matter,' said Kelly. 'Keep behind me and back me up. Don't draw your guns until I give the word. Leave the talking to me.'

The coach was soon upon them and Kelly moved her horse into the middle of the road and held up her hand.

'Whoa!' The driver pulled up the horses. The men before him did not hold guns and the youngest did not have a gun at all.

'Sorry to stop you,' said Kelly with a smile, 'but have you passed the prison wagon?'

'No, we haven't,' he said.

'I'd like to see if one of your passengers is a friend of mine,' she said, moving towards the coach door.

Kelly gave a small nod to her two companions and their guns appeared in their hands.

'Get down, and no tricks,' Hankins told them. He had been robbing coaches with Denver Branch and Quincey for longer than he'd spent with the Bassett gang robbing banks. What he was doing now was more in his line.

Kelly opened the coach door and indicated with a jerk of her thumb for the six passengers to alight. There were four men and two women. She helped the women down to the ground.

Hankins kept his gun on the driver and shot-gun rider and Jim Tobin came round to help Kelly.

'Sorry to have to do this to you, folks, but our needs are greater than yours. Empty your pockets and your purses and then go and sit over there,' she indicated the verge.

The men and women were smartly dressed and luckily for the gang, none wore a gun.

'Put the money on the ground and don't try anything,' Kelly warned.

'Huh!' one of the men exclaimed, as he felt in his pockets for money. 'You're nothing but a kid!' he snorted. 'In fact, I've an idea you're a girl! Is that right?'

'Depends what day it is,' Kelly replied, and Jim Tobin allowed one of his very rare smiles to cross his face.

Tobin ushered the men to sit down as requested by Kelly.

'What have you got for me, ladies?'

Kelly asked. 'I don't like robbing ladies as they've always been good to me in the past. I'll let you keep your trinkets, but any money will very gratefully accepted.'

The two women, who looked decidedly nervous, opened the strings of their small bags and both handed over what money they had. The older of the two went to remove her wedding ring.

'No need for that, ma'am. I've no use for a wedding ring.'

The coach driver and shot-gun rider still stood with their hands above their heads. Kelly could tell by their eyes that they were waiting for the opportunity to get even with the three. Kelly collected their rifles and found a gunbelt by the seat, plus a .45 pistol in the holster. They watched in fascination as Kelly put the gunbelt round her waist and adjusted the length of the gun drop to where her hand could reach it easily. It was obvious that this youngster was an experienced gunman — or woman.

Kelly looked for more shells for the weapons. They'd collected quite an arsenal, what with the two handguns and two rifles from the guards of the prison wagon and now two more rifles and a handgun from the coach. She found a box of shells for the rifles behind the driver's seat and jumped down with them. The money was collected up by Tobin while Hankins kept his gun aimed at the stomachs of the driver and shot-gun rider.

'Thanks a lot, ladies and gentlemen. We're most grateful to you. Enjoy the rest of the day. Goodbye!' Kelly called over her shoulder and the three galloped off, taking the right-hand road at the crossroads.

★ ★ ★

Steve Culley rode on until he came to a crossroads. A coach was stationary and he could see the passengers getting into it, assisted by the shot-gun rider, minus his shot-gun.

The men turned sharply at his approach and they noticed the young man was wearing a gun.

'Afternoon,' Culley called, as he drew up beside them.

'You're not another hold-up man, are you?' one of the passengers asked, putting his head out of the coach window.

'Me?' Steve asked in surprise. 'No. Why, have you just been robbed?' he asked.

'Sure have!' the driver exclaimed, his face as black as thunder.

'How many of them were there?' Steve asked.

'Three. Two men and a youngster — not sure if she was male or female.'

'I don't think he-she knew his-herself!' the passenger said in disgust.

'Has a prison wagon passed you?' Steve asked them.

'No. Why? Have some prisoners escaped from it?' the driver asked him.

'No idea. I thought I'd have caught up with it by now. Which way did the hold-up men go?' was Steve's next question.

'Right,' the driver informed him.

Steve was now in a dilemma. No one had seen the prison wagon and if it had kept to its scheduled route, it would have gone straight ahead. Yet the stage had just been hit by three men — or two men and a boy/girl. He shook his head and frowned. Surely that boy/girl couldn't have been Kelly? Or could it? But Kelly had been wearing a dress when he'd last seen her. If she had been one of the holdup gang then it would have been obvious that she was a woman.

Steve raised his hand in thanks and farewell to the occupants of the stagecoach.

He made a decision: he would trail the fleeing three who had taken the right-hand turn in the road. But what if he was making the wrong decision and was going on a wild goose chase? What if the prison wagon had indeed gone straight ahead? Then he would have missed the opportunity of reaching Kelly before she was put inside for ten years. There was nothing for it. He would leave it in the lap of the gods and ride the right-hand trail. Something deep in the back of his mind told him he was making the right choice.

8

After a night spent in the open and with only a horse blanket for each of them to keep out the night chill, the three travellers rode on again without even a cup of coffee to sustain them.

By noon they arrived at a town called Colfax. Jim Tobin was quick to notice the town had a bank. There was also a hotel and an outfitter's.

'I reckon we ought to get ourselves some new clothes,' said Hankins. 'The law will have our descriptions by now.'

'Maybe I'd better go back to being a woman again,' was Kelly's thought. 'It's a shame I wasted that good dress on that apology for a man back there.'

'Sure was,' said Jim, with just a hint of a smile.

Kelly flashed him a look. 'We'll put the horses up first and after we've bought some new clothes, we'll look more respectable when we book into the hotel for the night.'

Jim thought it over and said, 'We'll have to watch the money. We didn't collect all that much yesterday.'

'Well, we can't just book one room, with me in a dress with two men. We'll have to have two rooms. Maybe if I was Mrs James and you were Mr James, Jim, that would help with our disguise. You can be Mr James's brother, Hank James.'

'I don't know, Kelly,' Jim floundered.

'I'm not asking you to sleep with me!' Kelly snapped. 'As my husband you'll have to buy me a dress. If I go into the shop they'll remember what I look like now.'

'I can't go buying no women's dresses!' Jim exclaimed in disgust. 'Anyhow, I don't know your size.'

'Neither do I,' Kelly remembered. 'Just get them to hold it up then you'll have a fair idea. I'll be waiting for you both in the alley by the stables.'

Nearly an hour later, two smartly dressed men walked towards her as she sat on a bale of hay by the corral.

'One dress,' said Tobin, handing a parcel to her. 'Hope it fits.'

There was no one in the stables and Kelly took the parcel from him and went inside. Five minutes later a pretty young woman emerged. Hankins whistled. Tobin nodded.

Kelly kept the clothes she had been wearing and had wrapped them in the brown paper the dress had come in. She would need them again when they rode off the next morning. Her gun belt was hung with her saddle.

'I bought you a hat, too,' said Jim, 'but it's a man's hat for riding. It'll help disguise you when you go back to being a young man again.'

Kelly nodded her thanks. Jim held the hat in his hand as it would not have gone with her new attire.

'Let's book into the hotel and get something to eat. I'm starving,' Kelly said.

As they walked together, Kelly slipped her arm through Jim's like a wife would. Jim looked down at her and saw she still looked pale. She had been nauseous again before they had mounted up that morning.

Jim booked the three of them into their rooms and they were glad to find the hotel also did meals. Jim and Hankins had also kept their old clothes and all three deposited the parcels in the rooms before going down for something to eat.

As they sat at a table with a pure white linen cloth, Kelly felt she would always remember the meals she'd taken with Hay Bassett in Larkinton. After all that had happened to her, she was still in the company of two of the Bassett gang. She knew by now that the law would have realized that the prison wagon would not be arriving at the prison and there would be a search for it and its occupants.

All three were occupied with their own thoughts and hardly a word passed between them. Kelly thought about Steve and wondered if he was still working for Sarah Dobson at the restaurant in Hazelworth. How she wished he would have disregarded her order not to think of her again and to get on with his life without her. If only he would walk in that door right now and take her off with him somewhere where they could be alone at last. But the next thought came to her with a stab in her heart. He would hardly want her now after she'd killed the guards and held up a stagecoach. And definitely not after finding out that she was carrying his father's child.

Kelly took another mouthful of food and could hardly swallow it as she thought about him again. This would be the last time she would recall him to her mind. She resolved that from now on he would be part of her past, never her present or future.

'Shall we take a walk around the town afterwards?' Jim was saying, breaking into her thoughts.

'Mebbe we'd better lie low?' Hankins put forward.

'I reckon it's safe to risk it,' said Kelly. 'I'm tired of being hidden away.'

The three left the hotel, Kelly taking Tobin's arm again like a married couple, Hankins trailing after them.

They passed the bank and Kelly was aware that the two men by her side were taking more than a casual interest in the place.

'Let's get out of this county before we even consider doing another job, Jim,' Kelly said. 'We don't want to blaze a trail wherever we go and give the law a line on us so early on.'

'We might as well have a go while we're here,' Hankins chimed in.

'We'll do as Kelly says,' said Jim.

'Huh, so she's running this oufit now, is she?'

'She certainly is!' Jim told him in no uncertain terms. 'If it weren't for Kelly, I'd be swinging from a rope by now, and you would be starting a thirty-year stretch. You're getting on a bit in years now, Hankins; I doubt if you'd come out afore you died.'

Hankins grunted and continued his walk up the main street with the other two. He considered trying the bank job on his own, but then Hankins never did anything on his own.

After their evening meal at the hotel, Hankins and Tobin moved to the bar for a drink or two before retiring. Kelly took this opportunity of having a bath laid on for her in her room and was soon relaxing in the warm water. She washed her hair at the same time and realized that it was now almost shoulder length. She wondered whether to cut it shorter and remain in the guise of a boy or let it grow and wear a dress more often. If only she knew what would happen next. They had to get as far away as possible before being detected by the law. She realized that the three of them travelling together made it more likely for them to be identified and picked up. She didn't want any more killing, she had done enough already, and was under no illusions about her fate if she were picked up: she had killed two guards and that would mean the death sentence for her.

Jim Tobin knocked on the bedroom door before unlocking it. Kelly was already in bed, but not asleep. The lamp was lit by the bedside, the wick turned down low.

He began to undress down to his longjohns and picked up one of the pillows and a blanket and lay down on the floor.

'I guess it's a shame to waste half a bed,' said Kelly.

'It's OK. I'm used to sleeping on the ground,' was his reply. 'You can turn the lamp out now if you like,' he suggested.

Tobin slept on and off for an hour, but he could hear small sounds coming from the bed. It was obvious that Kelly was crying, yet trying hard for him not to hear.

'Anything I can do, Kelly?' the tall,

wiry man asked quietly. 'Are you crying?'

There was a sniff. 'Of course I'm not crying!' she told him vehemently. 'I never cry!'

'No, you're a hard little nut, ain't yer? But you can cry if you want to. I won't hold it against yer. Don't go taking this the wrong way, but if you'd like me to just hold you . . . ?'

There was no reply from that quarter.

'Guess not,' he said. 'It might lead to other things and we wouldn't want that, would we?'

Again there was no reply.

'Goodnight then,' said Tobin.

'Jim.'

'Yeah.'

'I'd like you to hold me — but *just* hold,' she emphasized. 'I'm not leading you on or nothing.'

'I understand.'

He picked up his pillow and the blanket and got under the covers. Kelly was wearing her drawers and a camisole and she snuggled against him like a little girl wanting comfort. He tentatively put an arm around her and felt her head on his heart. How he'd envied Hay Bassett when he'd taken her that first time at Kelly's old homestead. Sandy Kaye and Quincey had died trying to prevent him. Jim stroked her hair which felt shiny and clean after the wash and Kelly smelt of soap.

Neither of them spoke or moved. He felt her gradually falling off to sleep in his arms and was grateful for her trust in him. He knew he would never betray her trust. She had no idea what effect she had on men. Everyone who had met her had wanted her, it was obvious while they were up at Paradise. She had been the only woman among them all, yet she never flaunted herself before them. She had just stayed close to Hay Bassett for protection and even he betrayed her trust in the end. The girl was now paying a heavy price for it by carrying his child.

When Kelly awoke the next morning

she found that Jim Tobin had left her during the night to return to a hard bed on the floor. A smile crossed her lips. Despite what he had done in the past, Kelly knew he was a good man at heart, one of the few and far between.

9

Kelly and Jim were both dressed when Hankins knocked on the door at around seven. Jim opened it to him and the small man entered. His eyes went straight to the bed and then at Tobin.

'Did you have a good night, you two?' he grinned slyly.

Kelly answered for them. 'The bed was very comfortable. Was yours, Hankins?'

'Yeah, but it was a mite lonely without someone to snuggle up to.'

'Well, there you go,' said Kelly with a shrug of her shoulders and a forced smile. 'Seems like luck only comes to the good-looking ones.' She flashed Jim a quick smile and made for the door.

'Are we taking breakfast before we leave?' she asked. 'I only want coffee myself.'

'OK, that'll do for us, too,' said Jim.

'We'll need supplies,' Kelly reminded them. 'How are we for money?' she asked, as the three sat down at one of the tables.

Jim took the remainder of the coach hold-up money out of the breast pocket of his new coat. 'Forty dollars. We'll need bedrolls, coffee, flour, a skillet and mugs — plus some jerky I reckon for now.'

'Will that cover it?' Kelly asked, nodding her head towards the money.

'It ought to,' was Hankins' opinion.

'I'll pay the bill then we'll get it all. We didn't oughta all go together,' Jim suggested. 'We'll get some of it between us and make out we don't know each other. I don't think you should come with us, Kelly. Wait at the stables and change your clothes for riding while we're gone.'

Kelly nodded and left the hotel and the formalities of payment to be taken care of by Jim Tobin.

The two men entered the general

store separately and made their purchases, having decided which of them would ask for the different goods. Jim Tobin left the store first and made his way to the stables. Hankins followed him a moment or two later carrying the goods he'd purchased. Tobin was turning the corner when Hankins came out of the store. A rider was approaching the hotel and Hankins' heart lurched in alarm when he recognized who it was — Steve Culley! The small man stopped suddenly and turned his face towards the store window so he would not be recognized, and when Culley had dismounted and entered the hotel, Hankins hurried as fast as he could without actually running towards the stables.

Steve had spent the night in the open and when he came to the town of Colfax early the next morning, he decided he'd check the hotel register in case the three fugitives had booked in there. Not that they would have used their own names of course.

'Mornin',' said Steve to the hotel clerk. 'Have two men and a young woman booked in here?'

'You the law, mister?' the small, thin clerk asked suspiciously.

'Not exactly. I'm tracking three people and I thought they might come here for the night.'

The clerk looked at the register. 'There's a Mr and Mrs James and a Mr H. James.' He looked up at the enquirer.

'What do they look like?' asked Steve.

'Tall, thin man — Mr James. Pretty, young woman, younger than her husband, and the other Mr James — smallish, older man, Mr James's brother.'

'What colour hair did the young woman have?' asked Steve.

'I suppose you'd call it red.'

Steve's heart jumped slightly at this. It must be Kelly, Tobin and Hankins. It just had to be!

'Are they still around?' asked Steve. He was getting more excited by the minute at the feeling of being so close to Kelly once more.

'No — they left earlier on,' the clerk informed him.

'How long ago?'

'Not sure,' came the reply. 'Someone else was on the desk. I could find out if you like. I'll ask the other clerk before he goes off duty.'

'But it was this morning?' Steve asked urgently.

'Yes, this morning, earlier on.'

'I'm obliged,' Steve told him and hurried out of the hotel and remounted his horse. He was soon cantering away and guessed that the three would be continuing with their flight along the same road ahead, taking them further away from the crossroads where they'd held up the coach.

Hankins did not want to tell Kelly that Steve Culley was in town. He knew the young man would not be happy to meet up with him again after he and Quincey had hurt him so badly at the river by the Big B Ranch about four months ago. As the three, who had changed their clothes in the stables, mounted up, Hankins moved his horse forward in front of the others so he could keep a sharp eye out for Steve. As they reached the corner of the alley, Hankins saw Steve Culley riding out of town at a fast speed. He pulled up his horse, forcing Tobin and Kelly to make their own horses stumble slightly.

'What're you doing, Hankins?' Tobin asked a bit irritably.

'I just thought of something,' he said, in explanation of his sudden halt. 'We haven't decided where we're heading. We can't just ride aimlessly around without a definite destination.'

Kelly nodded in agreement. 'We must get into the next state as soon as possible. Any idea which one?'

'Wyoming's the nearest from where we are now,' said Tobin.

'And how far's that?' Kelly asked.

'Not sure. I reckon it'd be about one hundred and fifty miles.'

'And how long do you think it'd take

us to cover that?' she asked again.

'What do you reckon, Hankins?' Tobin frowned.

'Depends how far we travel each day, don't it? Mebbe ten to fifteen days is my guess.'

Both men looked at Kelly, who picked up their thoughts. 'You're wondering if I can keep up the pace for that long,' she said for them.

'Waal, we won't get anywhere if we don't start ridin',' Tobin remarked.

'Which way's Wyoming?' asked Kelly.

Tobin looked up at the sky. The sun was ahead of them, making that direction east.

'Left,' he said decisively. 'That's north.'

Kelly chuckled. 'Good job we've got you along, Jim.'

Hankins grunted. He was feeling decidedly left out of things, what with Tobin sharing a room, and a bed, with Kelly, and now being praised for his opinions. He was also worried about running into Culley. It was the last thing he wanted as he knew that young man would break up the three of them. He would either take Kelly away on his own or join up with the two, leaving him to fend for himself. If he could help it, he had no intention of that happening. Hankins knew he was no good on his own. All his life someone else had made the decisions for him and he would follow blindly.

By taking the left-hand road from the town, they would be backtracking to the crossroads where they'd held up the coach. But it couldn't be helped. The trail they wanted would be straight ahead at the crossroads.

Meanwhile Steve Culley had turned right as he left town. He had thought that the three would be keeping away from the crossroads, but as he rode on a thought came into his mind. Where would they be heading? The nearest state from there would be Wyoming, as Tobin had already deduced. They would try and get out of Colorado as fast as they could, so Wyoming was the most likely choice. Kentucky would be further for them to go and naturally take longer.

Steve pulled his horse to a stop and thought for a few more minutes. He would have to make his mind up quickly and not waste any more time. Yes, Wyoming was where they'd make for. He was sure of it.

He had no idea how much time he had wasted and how far ahead of him they were. Even now, he could have made a big mistake in changing course. But what else could he do except give up?

The three ahead of him tried to make up the time taken by spending the night at the hotel. They reached the crossroads after three hours' hard ride and noted that there was no one else on the road. A mile further on Kelly called a halt.

'You two go on ahead. I've got to make a stop.'

'We'll all have a breather,' said Tobin.

'I don't think you'll enjoy my

company during the next few minutes,' Kelly informed them, jumping from her horse and turning her head away from them. Tobin and Hankins rode off away before stopping themselves.

'This is getting to be a habit,' Hankins growled.

'The poor kid can't help it!' Tobin retorted.

'She ain't a kid no longer, she's a grown woman.'

'Yeah,' Tobin agreed, 'Bassett saw to that.'

'Seems like you two have got pretty pally since last night. What was she like, the little whore?'

Hankins was not prepared for what happened next. Jim Tobin's fist crashed into the small man's face, sending him reeling on to his back. Hankins' hand moved to his holster but Tobin's gun was already out.

'If you ever badmouth Kelly again I'll kill yer. And that's no idle threat. You won't ever meet a finer lady than her and that's the truth. She might try and sound tough, but deep down she's still only just a little girl, and you treat her with respect, savvy?'

Hankins got to his feet and was still in shock. 'As you say, Jim. As you say.'

Kelly took a drink from the canteen slung from the horse's pommel and looked down the trail they'd just travelled. A lone rider, just a dot in the distance was coming their way. She wondered if he was the law or just a drifter who happened to be going in the same direction. Maybe she'd better tell the others so they could keep on the alert.

She went to mount up and saw Hankins lying on the ground. Tobin had a gun in his hand, pointing straight at the man. She remounted quickly and jabbed her horse in the flanks with her heels. Within a minute or so she had reached the men. Hankins was now standing and Tobin had reholstered his gun.

'What's going on?' Kelly demanded.

'Just a bit of a disagreement,' Jim Tobin said.

'If we're gonna travel together, we've got to get along,' Kelly pointed out to them.

Tobin flashed Hankins another savage look and remounted his horse.

'We've got someone on our trail back there,' Kelly announced. 'Maybe nothing to worry about, just another traveller I guess. If it was the law then there would be more of them, wouldn't there, Jim?'

'I reckon,' the tall man said, pulling his mount's head round in the direction they were going to travel.

Hankins was quiet. Kelly would have liked to have known what the argument had been about. Was it about her? she wondered. She knew Hankins didn't think much of her. The feeling had rubbed off on him from her stepfather, Denver Branch. She rode with the two men and glanced at them from time to time, wondering if any more ill-feeling would erupt. She knew things would have been much better without Hankins. Jim Tobin had proved to her that she could trust him and she was aware that he respected her and maybe even more than that.

It was funny how things changed, Kelly thought to herself. She remembered the day that Hay Bassett brought her into Larkinton, the gang's hideout town after the rest of the gang had gone on ahead the night before. She remembered the men had been far from happy at the thought of a boy, as they'd thought she was then, being one of the gang. Jim Tobin and some of the other men's words came back to her. Sandy Kaye had grumbled that the gang didn't want kids in that outfit. Hay had pointed out that he himself was no more than a kid, but Kaye had retorted that he had proved himself. Jim Tobin agreed with Sandy and said, 'Our lives depend on speed — and being able to stay in a saddle for hours — not fainting all over the place like a woman.'

Tobin had also been involved in arranging the fight between young Sandy Kaye and Kelly. The man had certainly changed towards her since then, Kelly realized. Hankins, on the other hand, had not, and she had a nasty feeling inside her that things might go terribly wrong because of that man.

10

There was a full moon that night. Useful if someone needed to travel. Hankins took advantage of it.

The other two were asleep in their bedrolls and Hankins crept silently out of his own and packed it on to his horse. He put his hand over the animal's velvety nose to stop it nickering, and saddled up.

He moved out slowly at first, glancing quickly at the two sleeping figures by the now dead embers of the fire. They hadn't heard him. Soon he was cantering in the opposite direction from where the three were heading, retracing the trail they had covered the day before.

After a couple of hours, Hankins brought his horse to a slow trot. He could see the camp-fire ahead of him, tucked in among a stand of cotton-woods. Hankins moved his mount to one side so that he did not approach his quarry in a direct line. He had now reached the trees and dismounted, dropping the reins to the ground.

The man he was after was asleep in his bedroll and Hankins drew his gun and cocked back the hammer. The sound seemed surprisingly loud to him in the stillness. It made him wonder if the man on the ground had heard it.

The man had heard it but he was not in the bedroll. He had already heard the approaching rider some time back and had bunched the blankets up as if he was still inside them and retreated to the safety of the trees.

Hankins aimed his gun carefully for the centre of the bedroll and fired. The man he was after could not see him but saw the flash of his gun. The man was Steve Culley and he fired at the flash, not knowing if he had hit him or not. Another bullet was fired from the trees, proving that the bushwhacker was still alive, and this time Hankins scored: Steve Culley fell back and lay still.

Hankins waited for a moment but was certain that Culley now lay dead. He took his mount by the reins and led it towards the still body of the man who had been trailing them. Hankins gave Culley's body a kick but there was no response. A slow smile came to the small man's lips. They wouldn't be followed from now on.

★ ★ ★

Kelly awoke the next morning, a booted foot close by her head. Her heart lurched in her breast and her hand went straight for her gun in its holster by her side.

'It's OK, Kelly, it's only me.' It was Jim Tobin's voice.

She looked up and noticed Jim was holding a mug of coffee for her. He was gratified to receive a smile in thanks. 'Hankins has gone,' he informed her, as he sat on his haunches and handed her the mug.

'Gone?' she echoed. 'How long ago?'

'No idea. Sometime during the night.'

'Do you reckon he'll be coming back — or did that little set to between you yesterday make him feel unwelcome.'

'He didn't say he was leaving,' said Jim.

'I don't trust that man when he's here, and I don't trust him when he's not,' Kelly said between clenched teeth. 'What were you two arguing about yesterday, anyway? Was it anything to do with me?'

'It might have bin,' Jim stood up again and turned away from her, drinking his own coffee.

'I'd like to know,' Kelly continued.

'No you wouldn't. Forget it. I've got some beans heating,' he offered.

'I don't think so,' she replied. 'Are we gonna wait for him, or ride on without him?'

'When we've cleared up after breakfast I'll look around to see if he's within view. He coulda gone on ahead of us.'

There was no sign of Hankins and the two set off again without him. Later on in the day, however, they heard the sound of an approaching rider and a few minutes later Hankins rode up to them, a self-satisfied smile on his face.

'Where the hell have you bin?' Jim demanded to know.

'Looking after our backs, of course!' Hankins replied. 'I'm starving. When are we stopping for some grub?'

'You're too late, breakfast's over,' Jim grunted. 'Who did yer bushwhack back there?'

'Who said I bushwhacked him?' Hankins looked angry at the suggestion.

'Waal, you sure as hell wouldn't let him see you coming afore you plugged him,' Jim said grimly.

'Anyone'd think you were a preacher or somethin', Jim.' Hankins gave him a sideways look. 'You ain't so goddam innocent yourself!'

Jim sighed. This man was becoming a

105

thorn in his side and he fully understood why Kelly hated his guts.

'Who was it you killed anyway?' asked Kelly.

'He wore a star,' Hankins lied, 'so I did us all a favour. He won't be no loss.'

'What sorta star?' said Jim.

'Not sure. It was dark.'

Kelly's face looked as black as thunder. 'How do you know who you were killing if it was dark?' she asked him. 'He could've been anyone — just a drifter or something like that.'

'But he weren't!' Hankins flung back at her.

Tobin and Kelly knew it was no use pursuing the line of conversation. They would get nowhere with this man and they rode on again until noon. All three were glad of the stop.

* * *

Morning came for Steve Culley. His head hurt and he put his hand on the wet place above his left ear and saw it was covered with blood. There did not seem to be any other wound anywhere and he sat up and looked around him. He could not remember what he was doing in the clearing of the cottonwood trees. There were the ashes of a fire close by and a bedroll beside it. He went to stand up and everything around him seemed to spin. All went black as he collapsed.

The next time Steve Culley regained consciousness there was a man standing beside his prone body. His brain was too befuddled to ask himself if he was friend or foe and merely looked up at the tall man looking down at him, a US marshal's badge pinned to his shirt.

'What happened to you, Steve?' the marshal asked him.

'You know my name?' Steve muttered.

The marshal frowned. 'Of course I know your name. Who did this to you? It looks like a bullet crease above your ear.'

'I can't remember what happened,' Steve frowned.

'I reckon you're a bit concussed,' said the lawman. 'Come on, I'll help you to stand.'

Steve was helped to his feet but still felt groggy. He looked at the marshal's face but didn't recognize him.

'I don't know what I'm doing here,' said Steve. 'I've no idea where I was going or where I've come from — and I didn't know my name until you called me Steve.'

'It might come back to you after a while. Don't you remember me?'

'No,' Steve replied. 'Where did we meet before?'

'We first met in Hazelworth. We rescued your girl-friend, Kelly, from the Bassett gang.'

'Kelly?' Steve frowned. 'I don't remember no Kelly.'

Luke Dalton stroked his firm jaw and he, too, frowned. He wondered if Steve Culley was putting it on, pretending not to remember past events. For all he knew Culley could have been the one who had killed the guards and released the prisoners from the prison wagon. Although Sarah Dobson hadn't betrayed Steve's intentions of releasing Kelly, he had guessed by her furtive manner when questioning her that that was what Steve had set out to do.

'I'd better wash that crease in your skull,' the marshal said. 'Then mebbe your memory will come back. I hope it does for there's a lot I want to know.'

After the wound had been washed and Dalton had ascertained that the bullet had merely creased Steve's skull and was not too deep, the lawman had to decide what to do next.

'By rights,' Dalton began, 'you oughta be seen by a doctor. Trouble is, I can't really spare the time taking you to a town for one. I just hope you'll be able to ride in a few minutes. I reckon we're on the trail of the three who escaped from the prison wagon.'

'Prison wagon?' Steve asked.

'Yes. Kelly, Tobin and Hankins were

on their way to Clark County prison.'

Culley shook his head in bewilderment, but it hurt.

Dalton knew he was wasting valuable time but he had to give the young man chance to recover before they moved off. Unless he left Steve where he was to fend for himself he knew he would have to bring him along on the fugitives' trail.

The lawman gathered up some more kindling and relit the fire and soon had a pot of coffee on the boil. After he'd drunk from the marshal's one and only mug he had to admit that he felt a lot better, but his memory was still non-existent.

Dalton kicked the embers of the fire to make sure it was out and assisted Steve up into the saddle of his horse which Hankins had left behind.

'You OK, Steve?' Dalton asked, giving him a sideways glance.

'I'll let you know shortly,' Steve replied. 'Where are we heading?'

'After Kelly and the other two

escapees. I reckon they're heading for Wyoming.'

Steve shook his head again. 'I don't understand.'

'You will — in time — I hope,' was Dalton's reply.

11

Later on that day, Kelly and her two companions came to a river. They allowed the horses to drink and Jim called a halt for a while.

'It would be nice to go for a swim,' said Kelly.

'You can freshen up a bit, but we haven't time for relaxing,' Jim pointed out to her.

'What're you worrying about, Jim?' Hankins piped up. 'I got rid of that lawman way back. It wouldn't hurt to have a swim. I'm going to,' the small man announced.

'I said no!' Jim told him assertively. He flashed a look at Kelly, hoping she would back up his decision. Kelly's smile told him that she had no intention of arguing with him.

Seeing a river again sent memories flooding back to Kelly of the river near her old homestead and the first meeting with Steve Culley. As she knelt on the river-bank and splashed water over her face, she recalled how Steve and another cowboy had come across her naked, floating on her back in the water and quite unaware of their presence. The memory of further meetings beside the river came to her as vivid pictures in her mind.

'Are you ready, Kelly?' It was Jim Tobin's voice breaking into her thoughts.

She nodded and remounted her horse. The river was low at this point and the three riders crossed easily to the other bank.

'You were miles away just then,' Jim said.

'Yes,' she sighed. 'Miles away from here. At a place I'll never see again, and with someone I'll never see again.'

Tobin looked ahead of him. He knew who that someone was — Steve Culley. He guessed that man would always be at the back of her mind. He was surprised that he felt jealous.

* * *

Luke Dalton's brain had been constantly ticking away as he rode beside Steve Culley. He had a feeling that one of the three, either Hankins or Tobin, had been the one who had shot Steve. Whoever it was must have thought they'd killed him. He doubted now that Steve had been the one to release the three from the prison wagon. It had obviously been done before he came along or the four of them would be riding together. Unless of course there had been a falling out and Steve had been shot to get rid of him. Maybe they had fought over Kelly? There were all sorts of combinations to consider and he realized he would never know the truth until they met up with them.

Dalton figured the three were about two hours ahead of them. He glanced at young Culley again, hoping he would be able to keep up the pace.

The lawman had hoped to meet up with more federal agents. He had telegraphed ahead to Wyoming and was informed a posse would leave from there and others would be placed along the border. Having Steve Culley along might not be such a good idea. He would back Kelly against him if there came a showdown, but with the young man's mental state at the moment he would be useless to both sides.

'It seems as if Kelly was at the forefront when they held up a stage-coach at the crossroads back there,' Dalton jerked his thumb behind him. 'The three of them bedded down for the night at the hotel in Colfax. Kelly took a room with Jim Tobin as Mr and Mrs James. Hankins had a room on his own.'

Dalton glanced across at Culley. The young man's expression did not alter. It was as if he had been talking about complete strangers. The lawman realized that at that moment, to

Culley, they were.

Culley and Dalton came to the river. Dalton dismounted and examined the ground. There were the prints of three horses and also three sets of footprints. Their quarry were not far ahead. He guessed that Kelly could be slowing them down and now that Steve Culley had been shot and was presumably dead, they would not be quite so vigilant.

As Culley sat his horse and looked down at the water, his brain started to work. A river. Where had he seen a river before? Why was it of interest to him now? A leaf floated down stream and at that moment a memory flashed into his head. A girl with long red hair, floating on the water on her back, looking up at the sky. A beautiful young girl, naked.

After that, Culley's mind went blank again. But the vision of the girl remained.

Dalton allowed the horses to drink before the two of them crossed the river and followed the trail. There were three of the outlaws and only two of them following, only one not counting Steve Culley. He wondered how things would turn out. He knew he would have to catch them unawares, possibly at night, or there would be much bloodshed. He was not too worried what happened to Tobin and Hankins, but he did not want any harm to come to Kelly. He felt he had betrayed her by putting her up for trail. He had been certain she would have been let off. The sentence was far too harsh, especially after she had helped the law to find the outlaws' hideout after all those years. The only thing that had gone against her was helping Sandy Kaye escape after the bank raid. He realized with sadness that that kindly action on her part would probably be the last kind thing she would ever do — for anybody. She had been let down badly — by her stepfather, Denver Branch, by Hay Bassett in whom she had put her trust, and then the law. It was enough to turn a sweet, kindly girl into a hardened criminal. He was yet to find out what the two guards had attempted before she shot them.

'Any memories returned yet, Steve?' Luke Dalton asked his companion beside him.

'At the river back there — I seem to recall a beautiful young girl with long red hair. She was floating on her back and . . . she had no clothes on!'

Dalton suppressed a grin. A description like that would be hard to forget, he figured. He hoped that this was just one of the rest of his memories to emerge, hopefully before they reached the fugitives.

★ ★ ★

Night came and the three bedded down after a frugal supper. Tobin was becoming a bit worried about Kelly as she had hardly eaten anything over the last day or two. He knew what they had to offer wasn't exactly much to look forward to, but if she kept this up then she would be passing out on them. Hankins was already finding it hard to hide his annoyance with the girl.

The three may have settled down for the night, but Dalton and Culley had not. They were both riding throughout the night to reach the fugitives. They came upon them at around five in the morning.

Dalton touched Steve's arm and pointed ahead. 'Don't make a sound from now on, Steve,' Dalton warned. 'They're right ahead.'

It was as if Steve was having a dream. Everything seemed unreal. Why on earth was he trailing three people he did not know? It just didn't make any sense to him. He decided the only thing to do was to accept Dalton's judgement and do what the lawman told him to.

Dalton signed for Steve to dismount and the two dropped their horses' reins to the ground. The lawman withdrew his gun and pointed to Steve's own in its holster. Steve drew his own gun and followed the marshal quietly towards the sleeping trio.

Dalton indicated to Steve to stand still and hold his gun on them while he walked quietly around the three. He picked up Hankins' and Tobin's gun holsters lying beside them but he could not see one by Kelly's bedroll. Maybe she did not have one. He stood back a pace or two and yelled, 'OK you three, wake up!'

There were stirrings in the bedrolls. Tobin awoke first and his hand went for the missing holster. Hankins did likewise and was amazed that he could not find it.

Kelly opened her eyes. It was still dark, but morning was breaking in the east, giving some light. She knew the two men standing before them must be the law. Her own gun was inside the bedroll and her hand was on it. She would wait awhile to see how things panned out before resorting to using it.

'Kelly, come over here!' the lawman ordered.

Kelly remained in her bedroll. 'Is that you, Marshal Dalton?' she asked.

'It is — and Steve Culley.'

'Steve Culley?' It was Hankins' voice. 'But I thought I'd . . . '

'Killed him?' Dalton supplied the last words.

'Steve!' Kelly exclaimed.

The young man stood immobile, his gun still in his hand as the lawman had asked him to.

Kelly stayed in her bedroll. She did not want to betray the fact that she had a gun in her hand just yet.

'Hankins, you sidewinder! You knew who you'd shot at last night, didn't you?'

'So what?' Hankins flung back at her.

'But why?' Kelly asked. 'Steve isn't the law, he was just looking for me.'

'Huh!' Hankins scoffed. 'If it weren't for him, you wouldn't've run out on us looking for him and you wouldn't've let on to the law. Through you and him, Denver and Quincey died. They weren't much, but they were like my family, the only family I've ever had.'

'That's a poor excuse if ever I heard one,' Dalton told the man.

'Marshal,' Kelly began, 'I'm not coming back with you, I'm telling you straight. You'll have to shoot me — and my unborn baby, too.'

'You're expecting a baby?' Dalton asked in surprise.

'It's Bassett's,' Tobin informed him.

Dalton wavered slightly, but he had his job to do.

'Come on, Kelly, up you get,' Dalton told her quietly.

'I just told you, Marshal. I'm not coming with you. How are you gonna make me — knock me out or something?' Kelly goaded.

The lawman turned to Steve. 'Get her up, Steve!' he ordered.

Steve made towards Kelly after reholstering his gun.

Kelly sat up and a gun was held steadily in her hand.

'You've got no choice now, Marshal. You'll have to shoot me, or I'll shoot you.'

'She's pretty good at doing that!' Hankins spat.

Steve bent to take hold of her arm.

'What's the matter with you?' Kelly was perplexed at what was going on. As yet Steve had not spoken to her, or acknowledged her existence.

'Hankins' bullet grazed his skull and his memory's gone. It might not be permanent,' Dalton added.

Kelly looked from Steve to the marshal. 'You mean he don't recognize me?'

'Not yet.'

Kelly stood up unaided, her gun still in her hand as she stepped back a pace away from Culley.

'Put your gun down, Marshal!' Kelly ordered. 'I don't want to kill you, in fact I quite like you, but I will if you make me.'

Dalton hesitated a moment longer and let his firearm drop to the ground.

Tobin was nearest and quickly picked it up.

'It's no use going on any further, you three,' Luke Dalton told them. 'There are federal agents at the border and more coming this way. You might just as well come quietly.'

'No way!' said Tobin. 'I intend to live a bit longer. I've no intention of swinging in the breeze just yet.'

'How did you escape the guards?' Dalton wanted to know.

'Ask her!' Hankins jerked his thumb towards Kelly.

'Kelly had nothing to do with it,' Tobin stated. 'I killed the guards and we escaped.'

'Well, you've got nothing to lose, have you, Tobin?' said Dalton. 'By you confessing to it won't make no difference to your sentence. But it don't matter who did it, you're all implicated.'

Kelly sighed. 'That's what I thought you'd say. Well, if you want the truth, I killed them. My excuse is that they tried to rape me. I had no intention of letting them — and I'd do it again if ever the same thing happened. I've been used and abused by men too often and I've made my stand. The whole damn lot of you can go to hell!'

12

Steve Culley looked askance at the young woman before him. Her hair was the same red colour as that of the girl in the river, yet she looked a lot different. For one thing her hair was fairly short and she seemed older. He began to wonder how long ago it had been since he had last seen that girl in the river. Marshal Dalton had called her Kelly and said that she was Steve's girlfriend whom he had been searching for and that she had escaped from a prison wagon. Culley had heard her say that she was expecting a baby and that it was Bassett's. Who on earth was Bassett? All these questions buzzing around inside his head were beginning to annoy him. He wanted everything he had once known to come flooding back to him. He felt unable to act in the present circumstances. It was as if he was a puppet and Dalton was pulling the strings.

The woman before him could not possibly be his girlfriend. She spoke harshly and was obviously used to carrying a gun. She was also on the run from the law after escaping from a prison wagon.

The young man held his head with both hands, pressing his fingers into his skull above both ears.

Kelly still held the gun but it wavered a little as she saw the man she loved in such obvious torment.

'This is all your fault, Hankins! Just look at the state he's in! I oughta plug you right now.'

'Put yer gunbelt on, girl, and I'll put on mine. Let's get this over with once and fer all. Let's see if you can shoot a man holding a gun.'

Hankins picked up his gunbelt which lay at Dalton's feet and proceeded to put it around his hips and Kelly did likewise.

'Hankins, don't do it!' Tobin warned the man.

'Keep outa this, Tobin!' Hankins snarled.

Kelly had only just finished buckling on her gunbelt when Hankins' hand went for his gun. Against the odds, Kelly beat him to the draw and the spectators' mouths gaped open as Hankins fell forward, a bullet in his stomach.

At that moment past events flashed into Steve Culley's mind. He could remember a tall, powerfully built man grabbing another man's gun and firing towards him. He remembered firing back and killing him. But the man had not been aiming at him, but at another behind him — a large bear of a man with a black-bearded face. It came to Steve that the man he had killed had been his own father. Hay Bassett, the father of Kelly's as yet unborn baby, and the man Bassett had killed had been Kelly's stepfather, Denver Branch.

'I can hardly believe what I just saw!'

Dalton exclaimed. 'Who taught you to use a gun like that, girl?'

'I was taught by an expert — the father of my baby,' she replied quietly, but with pride in her voice.

Jim Tobin could see that Kelly had now reverted to the gentle, quiet lady — the other girl that he knew. She was two different women as he had already found out and was proud to know both of them. He knew that the memory of that beautiful hour he had lain with her before she gradually fell asleep in the hotel room in Colfax would remain with him for the rest of his life — however long or short that might be. In that hour she was his own little girl with whom he had shared special moments of innocence.

Kelly was aware that all three men's eyes were still upon her. She looked at Steve and wondered what was going on in that confused mind of his. There was no look of love in his eyes and Kelly was aware that she might have lost him forever.

Steve could not believe that this young woman standing before him, smoking gun in her hand, could possibly be the sweet, shy girl he had fallen in love with. She was a completely different woman and he felt no loving feelings towards her. How he wished everything could go back to normal, how it used to be, but he felt that the things that had happened since Kelly had said goodbye to him in the Hazelworth jail had come between them. He had lost her once when the Bassett gang had kept her with them and he was sure he had lost her again. She had spent far more time in other men's company than she had ever done with him. She was now hardened and could look after herself. She did not need him or anyone else to take care of her.

'I guess we'd better bury it,' said Kelly, jerking her gun in Hankins' direction on the ground. She replaced the gun in its holster which seemed to sit easily on her hip. 'Unless you need it for evidence, Marshal?'

Dalton felt uneasy without a gun and knew that Tobin or Kelly could easily kill him without any compunction. He knew he should have brought some men with him but they would not have had any jurisdiction outside the county line. Only he, as a federal marshal, had the authority of a judge and jury.

'I don't suppose you've brought a shovel with you, have you, Marshal?' Kelly asked flippantly.

'No, I haven't. We'll have to gather up stones and put them on the body to keep the buzzards off him.'

'Go on then,' said Kelly, 'start gathering. Meanwhile I'll fix some coffee and something to eat for us all.'

The three men moved off and started collecting large stones as the marshal had suggested and after the deed had been done, returned to the camp-fire where Kelly handed out mugs of coffee and some oatcakes.

'What happens now?' Luke Dalton asked the girl, who was obviously in charge of things at the moment.

'Well, as I said before, Marshal, I'm not going to prison. I've no intention of giving birth to my baby inside. And you're not taking Jim back either,' she told him forcefully. 'True, Jim's been an outlaw, like me, but deep down he's a good man. He's proved that to me.'

'But you're not the law, Kelly,' Dalton reminded her. 'I am, and I have to uphold it.'

'Huh!' Kelly scoffed and shook her head in disbelief. 'Like that judge in Hazelworth? You know it and I know it, he gave an unfair decision, about me at least. I didn't deserve ten years. I shoulda bin given a medal or something for helping to bring in the Bassett gang. A lot of thanks I got for that! I wish now that I hadn't. I didn't enjoy my life with the gang, but I might just as well have stayed with them given the outcome for me.'

Dalton was sitting on the ground, cross-legged and drinking his coffee. He regarded the girl between sips. He had to agree with her. If she had been let off she would not have killed the guards on the prison wagon and would not have had the need for money, forcing them to rob the stagecoach.

'I've got a proposition for you, Marshal,' Kelly began.

'Oh,' Dalton said hesitantly, 'and what's that?'

'I want to make a bargain with you.' Kelly ate some oatcake and Jim was glad she was eating something for a change.

'I don't make bargains,' Dalton told her emphatically.

'Well you'd better,' said Kelly.

Dalton thought for a minute and was interested to know what was on this girl's mind.

'I'll give you your gun back,' she began.

'No, Kelly, don't!' Tobin warned her.

She disregarded his warning.

'First of all, you've got to give me your word you'll keep to the bargain we make. Do you?' she asked the lawman.

'I can't give my word on something I don't know about,' he told her.

'Give me your word you'll abide by the bargain I'm gonna make with you!' Kelly demanded of him.

Dalton thought for a few moments more, then nodded reluctantly.

'Say it out loud, Marshal. Say that you give me your word. You're a fair man and I know you'll keep to it.'

'OK, Kelly, I give you my word — whatever you have in mind. I can't do no other with you and Tobin armed and me unarmed.'

Kelly flashed him a smile.

'Now this is the bargain. I'm gonna give you back your gun and you and I have a shoot-out. If you kill me, Jim goes free. Do you promise to agree to that part of the bargain?' Kelly looked up at the marshal's face to see if she could guess his reaction, but his expression was inscrutable.

'I can't promise that, Kelly,' Dalton told her.

'But you promised you'd agree to

what I said!' she stormed.

'OK, you have my word on it. What's the next part? There is a next part, isn't there?'

'The next part is, if I shoot you, then Jim and I both go free.'

'Waal, that's fairly obvious, girl! If you shoot me, of course you'll escape. It'll just leave another corpse on your list of crimes.'

Kelly's face looked angry. 'Do you consider that killing Hankins was a crime?' she demanded to know.

'It was a fair fight, and you won. I'm kinda worried that you might win again.'

'Where's your guts, Marshal?' she said. 'Taking on a little woman.'

'Some woman!' Luke Dalton replied tersely. 'OK, let's get it over with — one way or another. I agree to your terms, young lady.'

'Give him his belt, Jim,' said Kelly.

It was handed over reluctantly and Tobin covered the man with his own gun until the marshal had fastened the buckle and set the belt on his hips to his satisfaction. Then Tobin replaced his own gun and waited.

The tall, well-built marshal stood about twelve feet away from the small young woman. It was an odd sight to the onlookers, Tobin and Culley. Steve began to believe he was dreaming again and this was not actually happening.

'OK, Marshal, when you're ready.' Kelly's arms were held loosely at her sides. There seemed to be no tension about her. It was as if what she was anticipating was of such little consequence as being forced to swat away an irritating fly.

Dalton watched the girl's eyes, which told him nothing. She had indeed been taught by an expert, professional gunman. She must have spent many hours practising, was the thought going through his mind.

Then the moment came. There was only one explosion and the two onlookers watched mesmerized as Dalton's gun spun out of his hand. The lawman's face contorted in pain as he gripped his bloody palm with his other hand.

'Use his bandanna to bind it up with,' Kelly told Steve.

Steve moved slowly, as if in a dream.

'Hurry it up!' Kelly told him irritably. 'He'll lose a lot of blood.'

It went through Jim Tobin's mind that that was the whole idea.

Dalton was in great pain and rocked from side to side, gripping his palm tightly, trying not to cry out.

'Did you intend shooting me in the hand — or did the bullet go astray a bit?' Dalton asked her through clenched teeth.

'Oh, I intended aiming for your hand, Marshal. In the bargain I made, I said, 'If I shoot you'. I had no intention of killing you — or I would have. Sorry your shooting hand's out of action. I hope it gets better soon. And don't forget the bargain you made with me. Jim and I are free to go and you won't be following us — will you?'

137

Steve bound up the marshal's hand as best he could, but the blood was still pouring from the wound.

'Have you got any whiskey in them saddle-bags, Marshal?' Kelly asked the lawman.

'No, 'fraid not.' He knew why she wanted it — to anaesthetize and cleanse the wound.

'I don't want you to bleed to death,' Kelly said, with obvious concern. 'We need some clean cloth.' They could see she was thinking.

'I don't want to do this, but it's urgent,' she said, walking over to the saddles on the ground by the horses. She took out the package done up in brown paper and undid the string. The men saw her tearing at the white petticoat beneath the dress she was so proud of, the one Jim Tobin had chosen for her from the store in Colfax.

She came back to them and removed the bloody bandanna. The bullet had gone straight through the palm of the lawman's right hand and out the other side. She inspected it and could see that it was a clean wound. Kelly poured some water over the palm and the back of it and quickly tied the strips of her petticoat firmly around his hand, finishing off with a knot.

'I'm real sorry about this, Marshal,' Kelly said sincerely. 'I hope it don't get infected. I'll give you some more of my petticoat for when the bandage needs changing.' She returned to the parcel and tore off some more strips from the bottom of her undergarment.

'Well, this is goodbye,' said Kelly after the breakfast things had been cleared away. 'Are you coming with us, Steve?' she asked hopefully, but deep down she knew what the answer would be.

13

Jim Tobin left them and walked towards the horses and started saddling his own and Kelly's mount.

Steve Culley shuffled his feet slightly. He had lost and found this young woman twice and now he was hesitating about following her.

'I reckon we said our final goodbyes in Hazelworth, Kelly,' was his answer.

She lowered her eyes and Culley could see her lower lip tremble slightly.

'I guess you don't love me any more?' she asked him.

'I've got my memory back, but you're no longer the girl I fell in love with. I'm not blaming you. Things have happened to alter all that.'

She nodded. 'I understand, Steve. I still love you though. Will you kiss me goodbye?'

He stepped forward and gave her a

brief kiss on her lips. 'Goodbye, Kelly. Good luck. I hope you have your baby OK.'

Kelly turned and raised her hand in farewell. 'Goodbye, Marshal. Sorry about the hand. But it coulda bin worse.'

The two men watched as Kelly walked towards the horses carrying her bedroll and the coffee pot.

Jim Tobin mounted his horse and pulled the animal's head towards the marshal and Steve. He drew up to them.

'Are you coming, Culley?' he asked.

Culley shook his head. 'Three's a crowd, I guess.'

'It needn't be,' he answered. 'I'd go on alone if you joined up with her.'

'No,' Steve shook his head.

'You're a durned fool, Culley. That girl loves you. You're the only one she's ever loved. Oh, well, it's your loss. You're giving up the finest woman there is.'

Tobin turned to the marshal. 'That

141

girl' — he jerked his thumb towards Kelly — 'saved my life and she saved yours, too, Dalton. Be thankful she only aimed at your hand — and I'm trusting you to keep your word that you won't follow us.'

Dalton nodded. 'I've given you my word, Tobin. But that don't mean that others won't be looking out for the two of you. You won't be safe even when you get to Wyoming. Kelly shouldn't be riding every day in her condition either.'

'I know that,' replied Tobin, 'but there's not much else we can do, is there? S'long the both of you!'

He cantered off to join Kelly, glad that Culley would not be joining her.

Steve and Dalton watched until they were nearly out of sight.

'Are you sure you've made the right decision, Steve?' Luke Dalton asked the young man.

'Mebbe not, Marshal. But she no longer needs me. She's well able to take care of herself, as she's proved.'

'It looked that way,' Dalton sighed, 'but deep down, she's not so tough. I reckon Tobin's pretty fond of her. He'll look out for her I dare say.'

* * *

Steve and the marshal arrived back in the town of Colfax two days later. Dalton made straight for the telegraph office where a message was awaiting him from Hazelworth.

TWO BODIES DISCOVERED AT BOTTOM OF RAVINE STOP UNIDENTIFIABLE STOP ONE WEARING DRESS STOP BOTH BODIES SHACKLED STOP UNABLE TO RETRIEVE BODIES FOR IDENTIFICATION STOP

Dalton read the telegraph message through twice. Anyone other than him reading it would immediately think that the body in a dress would be that of Kelly and the other one would therefore

143

be one of the prisoners. Someone had obviously worked it out well and intended that this would be the obvious conclusion. He wondered if it had been Kelly's plan.

Dalton thought for a few minutes and then sent a message of his own:

FORCED TO KILL PRISONER HANKINS STOP BODIES THOSE OF FEMALE PRISONER KELLY AND TOBIN STOP WHERE-ABOUTS OF BODIES OF TWO GUARDS UNKNOWN STOP

Dalton checked the message before it was transmitted. He felt guilty that he was misleading the law, but he knew he owed it to Kelly. No one would be looking for her and Tobin any longer, but unfortunately they would not know that. They would keep running. He had kept his part of the bargain and hoped the subject would now be closed.

Steve had booked two rooms at the hotel, one each for himself and the marshal and when the lawman returned from the telegraph office they both sought out a doctor.

Steve was pronounced fit but told to take things easy for a while.

'Well now, Marshal,' the doctor began, as he took the lawman's bandaged hand in his. 'Lucky you had some clean bandages with you, Marshal. Looks as though it's from a woman's petticoat?'

Dalton looked slightly embarrassed. 'Just something I happened to have in my saddle-bags,' he explained sheepishly.

'Hm,' said the doctor, as he began to inspect the wound. 'It's a bit inflamed, but if you put this ointment on it for a week and keep it clean, it should be all right. Can you move your fingers?'

Dalton tried wriggling his fingers but he was unable to do so. It felt numb.

The doctor 'hmmed' again. 'I hope there's no permanent damage, Marshal. See how it goes and come back and see me again.'

'I've got to get back to Hazelworth, Doc. I'll see a doctor there.'

'Right you are. Don't go trying to use a gun for a while.'

Dalton smiled slightly. 'I hope I don't have to. Thanks, Doc.'

The two men made their way back to the hotel and ordered lunch. It was the first time they were able to converse properly since they arrived in town.

'What did the telegraph say, Marshal?' Steve asked him.

'What I tell you now, Steve,' the lawman began, 'is strictly between you and me. Understand?'

Culley frowned and nodded. 'Whatever you say.'

'They've found two bodies at the bottom of a ravine but they're unable to get them out. Both were shackled and one was wearing a dress.'

Steve was quiet as thoughts buzzed around in his brain.

'They think it was Kelly, don't they?' he asked.

'Yes, and as they won't be retrieving

the bodies I confirmed that they were Kelly and Tobin and told them that I had to kill Hankins.'

Steve nodded his understanding of the matter. 'Nobody will be looking for them then from now on?'

'That's right. Pity I can't let them know that.'

As the two men ate their meal they discussed what would happen next. Steve had decided to look for work on a ranch somewhere. There would be too many memories for him back in Hazelworth, despite the happy time he had spent there in the town.

'What about you, Marshal?' Steve began. 'You won't be able to use your gun hand for a while.'

'If ever again,' Dalton replied. 'I reckon it's about time I retired anyhow. Might even consider tyin' the knot.'

Steve's mouth opened wide and he started to laugh. 'I thought you were a confirmed bachelor!'

'Hmm,' he mumbled. 'Gets a mite lonely at times.'

'Got anyone in mind?'

'Could be,' a tiny smile flickered over his lips.

'It wouldn't be a certain lady who runs a restaurant in Hazelworth, would it? I know she's bin sweet on you for ages.'

'Could be,' the marshal repeated.

Steve laughed out loud again. 'You couldn't do better that Sarah Dobson.'

Dalton nodded. 'That's what I thought.'

★ ★ ★

Jim Tobin looked across at Kelly as they rode. A tear splashed down on to her hands now and again as she held the reins, but she made no sound. He knew only too well that she was wishing that Culley was with her instead of him and wondered if she'd ever get the young man out of her mind.

They rode along in silence for a full hour and Tobin was aware that they were getting slower and slower. He would have liked to have urged Kelly on but decided to let her go her own pace.

'Are you OK?' he asked at last.

'Yes,' was her brief answer.

'Do you want to stop a while?'

'No.'

He would have liked to have held her just then and comforted her, but knew she only wanted comfort from Steve Culley. He began to feel irritated. They continued to ride for another couple of hours and the silence was becoming unbearable.

'We'll make a stop now,' Jim said, and Kelly dismounted immediately, but her legs felt wobbly when she reached the ground and they gave way beneath her.

Jim rushed towards her and knelt down beside her.

'I don't know what happened,' she said, sitting up.

'Lie down and rest,' he suggested. 'All this riding is getting too much for you.' He untied her bedroll from the cantle and laid it out. 'Take a nap for an hour and I'll get some food started.'

'Jim,' she began.

'Yeah?'

'You're very nice.'

He grinned and turned away in embarrassment and started building a fire.

14

Kelly and Jim made camp that night within sight of a farm of some sort. They could see in the distance smoke from a chimney and a line of washing blowing in the breeze.

Jim had considered calling in and asking if they needed workers to supplement the last of the remaining hold-up money, but thought better of it. The marshal had warned that federal agents would be on the lookout for any strangers in the vicinity. Jim allowed themselves a fire that night which would be obscured by a coppice of trees.

Kelly cleared away the dishes and mugs, allowing a small quantity of water to rinse them out. She had brightened up somewhat after the nap she had taken at noon that day and appeared to have forgotten about Steve

Culley. No doubt thoughts of him would return to her in her bedroll that night. Jim knew there was nothing he could do about that.

'Will you hold me tonight, Jim?' she asked him, as she settled down under the blankets. Tobin's bedroll had been placed some distance from her.

'I wish it was me you really wanted, Kelly,' he replied a little bitterly.

'It is you I want, Jim,' she said.

'I don't think it's such a good idea,' was his reply.

'Why isn't it?' she demanded to know.

'You know damn well why!'

Kelly went quiet. After a while she got up from her blankets and brought them over besides Jim.

'I'll come to you then,' she said. 'Hold me!' she ordered.

'You know how I feel about you, girl. Don't tease me. It ain't fair. You oughta know once a man gets roused it's hard for him to hold back.'

'You did back in Colfax,' she reminded him.

'I didn't stay with you all night, or hadn't you noticed?'

'Yes, I'd noticed.' Neither spoke for a while until Kelly continued, 'Jim, am I your woman now?'

He did not answer immediately. 'I don't know, are you?'

'Do you want me to be?'

'Not while you're really someone else's,' was his answer. 'Shut up and go to sleep.'

Kelly smiled to herself. She knew she was getting under his skin. It would only be a matter of time before she had broken down his defences.

'I want to be your woman, Jim,' she told him. 'If I was, then it wouldn't be wrong for you to sleep in my blankets.'

Jim Tobin growled. 'OK, you asked for it, Kelly. Don't go holding me back once I've started though as I won't be able to. Do you understand me?'

'I guess I do.' She sounded a little unsure of herself now and perhaps a bit afraid.

Jim Tobin pulled off his clothes and

lay down beside her. Kelly was fully dressed except for her boots.

As he started to unbutton her shirt she began to have second thoughts about what she had started. She had been naïve in thinking that a man could just hold her and nothing else. Once perhaps, but not twice.

He pulled down her pants and drawers, untangling them from her feet and threw them to one side.

'Hold me first,' she implored. 'Just hold me.'

She noticed that his breathing was becoming heavier and for a while he lay beside her and held her naked body to his own. He had never kissed her before and soon he found that her lips were like wine and he wanted more and more until he felt intoxicated.

Unlike Hay Bassett, Jim Tobin took his time. His fingers found all the little places on her body that made her want to cry out for him to take her completely.

His lovemaking was gentle and

sensuous and far more wonderful than Hay Bassett's had been. After Bassett had made love to her she had always felt ashamed and dirty. With Jim, it felt right. Jim did not want to hurt her as he was aware of the baby growing inside her belly.

Eventually he pulled away from her, satisfied.

'Jim . . . I am your woman now.'

'You sure are,' he answered. 'A real woman. Now I can feel that the baby inside you is mine. Thank you for letting me love you, Kelly.'

Her hand caressed his face and black hair. 'I love you, Jim Tobin. I really do,' she declared.

'Good, 'cos I love you too. Now go to sleep, you little minx!'

Kelly giggled and snuggled up against him, completely satisfied.

★   ★   ★

Morning came. Jim Tobin lay beside her, his elbow was on the ground and

155

his head was propped up on his open hand. Kelly was still asleep and he looked down at her beautiful face. He could hardly believe what had happened between them the night before. He felt lucky she had really wanted him. He was well aware that if he had attempted anything against her will, she would probably have shot him by now. He only hoped that it had really been him that she had made love to and had not had Steve Culley on her mind at the time. He had a feeling though that she really had erased Culley from her mind last night.

Jim got dressed and started a fire for the coffee pot. 'Come on, lazy bones!' he said, giving her a gentle nudge with his boot.

She opened her eyes and Tobin was greeted with a big smile.

'I'm mighty glad I saved you from the hangman, Jim Tobin,' she said.

'No more glad than I am! Ain't it good without Hankins?'

'Don't mention his name again,'

Kelly shook her head.

After a brief wash and clearing away the dishes, they were off again. They had no idea how much longer it would take to get to Wyoming and after another day's ride Kelly began to think that they would never reach that state. What if they had been riding in circles? she thought to herself. But she trusted Jim's judgement and left it all to him.

Down in a valley they could see a town. Jim wondered if they had now arrived in Wyoming, but realized they had not travelled long enough for this. He thought about risking going into town to replenish their supplies which were getting low. Perhaps if they donned their good clothes they wouldn't be suspected of being the fugitives? Perhaps if he went in alone and left Kelly on the outskirts? He would ask Kelly's opinion.

'It'd be nice to sleep in a comfortable bed again,' said Kelly — 'and to take a bath.'

Jim nodded. 'You deserve a bit of

comfort, Kelly. If only we had a place of our own.'

Kelly was quiet for a minute or two and then said, 'There is one place we could go . . . maybe.'

Tobin looked at her, wondering what she had in mind.

'What if we went back to Paradise? There's a cabin there — and water. There's game in the valley and a pool to swim in. In fact if we got in more supplies, we'd have everything we needed.'

'Wow!' Jim exclaimed. 'That's a thought. But it's a hell of a way back. We're nearer to Wyoming now than Paradise.'

Kelly sighed. 'Yeah, I know. It was a nice thought though, weren't it, Jim?'

'Yeah, it was, a real nice thought. Mebbe if you weren't expecting, things would be different. I'll get a job of some kind and build up some money, then we'll see how things pan out.'

They came closer to the town and Kelly made the decision that they would put on their best clothes and go into town. They would spend one night there at least, and see how much money they'd have left for more supplies.

* * *

The town was called Brewster and at that moment the sheriff was sitting in his office with his booted feet on his desk. He had just been handed a telegram informing him that the three prisoners who were being escorted to Clark County Prison were now dead. Three less for him to look out for. The lawman tore up the three wanted posters giving descriptions of the felons and tossed them into a waste-paper basket beside him.

* * *

The town of Brewster was smaller than Colfax, but it did have an hotel and a general store. Kelly and Jim dismounted outside the hotel and Kelly stayed with the horses.

'Who are we this time?' Jim asked her quietly before he went inside.

'What about Mr and Mrs Bassett?'

Jim was not too keen, but it was as good a name as any, he supposed, especially as Kelly was carrying Bassett's baby.

As Kelly waited for him to return and to take their belongings up to their room, she looked about her. It would be so nice to belong somewhere like this and be safe and contented. Her thoughts were interrupted by someone beside her on the boardwalk.

'Hello, Kelly. It is Kelly, isn't it?'

She turned to face the speaker and her mouth dropped open in surprise.

15

Seeing him standing there brought it all flashing back into her mind. It seemed so long ago now, but it could only have been about four months since that evening in Larkinton when Sandy Kaye and Jake Thomas had dragged her from her hotel bedroom and into the street outside the saloon. She recalled the fear she had felt and her rapid heartbeats as most of the Bassett gang surrounded her. Jim Tobin took bets on how long she would survive Sandy Kaye's blows before becoming unconscious. A smile came to her lips as she recalled how well she had fought back, causing Kaye quite a bit of damage to his face and to his manhood. She could hardly believe that she had allowed the man who had taken bets on that one-sided fight to make love to her the night before. But Jim Tobin was now a different man

161

from the one in Larkinton, and their excuse had been that he and the others had thought she was a boy anyway, plus the fact that most of them were drunk.

She came quickly back to the present day. 'Doc Reynolds?' she asked.

'Yes. I wasn't sure you'd remember me as you were hardly conscious when I examined you after that fight with Sandy Kaye. You put up a good show though, didn't you?' he smiled at her. 'What are you doing here, anyhow?' he asked. 'The judge obviously saw sense and let you go free.'

'Don't you believe it, Doc!' Kelly exclaimed. She looked about her and spoke quietly. 'I think it's best that we're not seen talking together here. Can I meet you somewhere — tonight perhaps when it's dark? I'd like to talk to you.'

'Of course,' the doctor nodded. 'I live in a room above the barber shop just down the street,' he nodded his head to his left. 'I'll be waiting for you when it gets dark. I hope you're not in any trouble?' he asked her.

'I'll let you know tonight. Goodbye for now, Doc.'

Reynolds touched his hat to her and walked on down the street.

He had only gone a few yards when Jim Tobin came out of the hotel. 'That's settled,' he informed her. 'Bring in our stuff and put it in our room. Then I'll take the horses to the stables.'

Kelly carried her saddle-bags and her parcel of riding clothes, plus the coffee pot and Jim brought in things of his own.

'How are we off for money, Jim?' Kelly asked when they had reached their room up the stairs.

'By the time we've paid for the room, meals and bought some supplies, we'll be dead broke.'

Kelly looked serious. She didn't fancy holding up another stage or even a bank. She hoped those days had gone now.

'I wonder if we can get some work in town?' she said, sitting down on the bed after dumping the things she'd carried on to the floor up one corner.

'I could ask around.'

'Maybe I could get work here in the hotel — wait on tables or something. I did it for a month at the restaurant in Hazelworth before my trial. I enjoyed it.'

'Sure you did, with Culley working alongside you.'

Kelly did not like Jim's tone. Would he always have a jealous streak in him where she was concerned? she wondered.

'I would have enjoyed it in any case,' she retorted, and Tobin caught the dark look she gave him.

'I'll put the horses in the stables,' he said, and left her in the room.

She realized that she had not told him about Doc Reynolds being in town and would do so when he returned. When he did return, however, Kelly had fallen asleep on top of the bed. She had no idea how long she had lain there before Jim woke her up.

'Shall we get some grub?' he asked. 'My stomach's growling.'

She noticed that while she had slept he had shaved and plastered down his hair with water. He looked a lot younger when he had shaved.

'Have I slept for long?' she asked him, but guessed she must have done for she felt much better for it.

'About an hour, I should imagine. I wish we could hang around here for longer. You shouldn't be riding every day in your condition,' Jim told her with obvious concern.

'I'll be OK,' she smiled. 'Let's get something to eat.'

★ ★ ★

When evening came, Kelly remembered her meeting with Doc Reynolds. She stepped out of the bath that had been laid on for her and Jim got into it in her place.

'I saw Doc Reynolds this morning when we arrived. You were booking us in here at the time. I forgot to tell you.'

'I wouldn't have thought you'da forgotten that!' he said in disbelief.

'Well I had,' Kelly replied. 'I said I'd meet him tonight where he's staying. I didn't want anyone to see us talking.'

'What's he doing here?' said Jim.

'I didn't have time to ask him. I'll find out later.'

'You're not to go!' was Jim's order. 'The less we see of anyone from Larkinton, the better. We don't want to be associated with any of them. In any case, if ol' Reynolds has a few drinks too many, his tongue might start wagging.'

Kelly could see his point, but did not actually say that she would not visit him.

Jim decided to go to the saloon for a drink after supper and expected Kelly to remain in their room and await his return. This, however, was not Kelly's intention. She objected to being told what she could or couldn't do by any man.

When Jim had been gone half an hour, Kelly slipped out of the hotel and made her way along the sidewalk. She hadn't gone far when a man lurched into her, obviously drunk.

' 'Evenin' miss. Have you got a little kiss for me?' He held her arms and pulled her towards him.

'Get off me, you're drunk!' she growled.

'Come on, now. Be nice to me.'

'Leave me alone — or you'll regret it!' Kelly informed him with conviction in her voice.

A man came along and intervened. Kelly's heart lurched when she noticed a star on the man's vest.

'Sorry, miss. I'll see to this,' said the sheriff. 'I'll take him to the jail to sleep it off for the night.'

'Thank you, Sheriff,' Kelly replied with a smile.

'What's a young woman like you doing out on the streets at this hour?'

Kelly looked surprised. 'Why, isn't it allowed, Sheriff?'

'Of course it's allowed, but it isn't wise for an unescorted woman to be wandering the streets at night. It's just a warning, that's all.'

'Thank you for your concern, but I'm not 'wandering'. I'm just visiting a friend — if I may?'

The sheriff had snapped the handcuffs on the drunk but he kept his eyes on Kelly.

'You look kinda familiar to me. I seem to recall seeing a picture of you somewhere.'

Kelly's heart started to pound. She realized she should have heeded Jim's warning and stayed in the hotel.

'I must have one of those ordinary faces that look like a lot of other women,' Kelly smiled again, but in reality did not feel like doing so.

'Huh!' the sheriff grinned 'Your face is far from ordinary, miss. Anyhow, you couldn't possibly be the one on the Wanted poster because I've been informed that that particular young woman is dead, along with her two companions in crime.'

'Really?' Kelly asked, interested now. 'What did they do, Sheriff?'

'Murder and bank robbery. The woman and one of the prisoners — Tobin I think his name was — were killed when the prison wagon went down a ravine. A US marshal killed the other one — Hankins as far as I can recall.'

'There you are then, Sheriff. Fancy me looking like one of those criminals! It's quite awful!'

The sheriff laughed. 'It was foolish of me to even consider you could possibly be a criminal, miss. I should make sure you do your visiting in daylight hours in future though. I wouldn't want anything to happen to you.'

'You're very kind, Sheriff. By the way, would you know if I can get some kind of employment in town?'

'What kind of thing are you after, miss?'

'I've waited on tables a while ago, but I've been taking care of my sick parents

169

for a year now. Unfortunately they both died within a month of each other.' Kelly looked suitably crestfallen and the sheriff fell for it.

'Sorry to hear that, miss. You might like to try the hotel,' he suggested.

'Thank you, Sheriff. You're very kind. I'll do that in the morning. I'm on my way to my aunt's in Wyoming, but I need to get some money together as my parents left me almost destitute.'

Brewster's lawman was by now completely captivated by this pretty young woman who was obviously in some distress. He would keep an eye out for her and try and help if he could.

Jim Tobin pushed open the batwing doors of the saloon and stepped out on to the boardwalk. He dodged back inside when he saw Kelly speaking to someone keeping hold of a drunk in handcuffs. What on earth was Kelly up to? He had told her to stay in the hotel yet here she was talking to the law.

He watched as the sheriff led the drunk away and Kelly proceeded down the street. He let her go on a bit and followed her. It suddenly dawned on Tobin that he could not trust the girl, even though they had been so close the night before. He did not like how he was feeling and it bothered him.

Kelly knocked on the door she had been told was the residence of Doc Reynolds. Tobin saw her enter and the door closed behind her.

16

Doc Reynolds opened the door to the expected knock and ushered Kelly ahead of him as he closed it behind him.

'It's good to see you, Kelly,' he said brightly. 'How are you?'

'I'm pregnant, Doc,' she said bluntly.

'Oh dear . . . Bassett's I expect?'

Kelly nodded. 'It's not what I wanted, but there's not much I can do about it now, eh?' She forced a smile which did not fool Reynolds.

'How far gone are you?' he asked her, indicating that she sit down on one of the easy chairs.

'Two months I guess.'

Reynolds stroked his short grey beard, obviously considering a possible solution.

'Have you thought about . . . getting rid of it, Kelly? There is some risk involved, of course,' he added quickly.

Kelly's mouth opened slightly. Reynolds could see that she had never even considered this.

'It'd be wrong, Doc. I don't think I could do that.'

Reynolds nodded emphatically. 'I shouldn't have even mentioned it. Forgive me.'

He walked towards the iron range and picked up the coffee pot. 'Coffee?' he asked her.

Kelly nodded. 'That would be nice — I think,' she added. 'I haven't been able to keep much down lately and haven't eaten much either.'

'Well that won't do. You must keep your strength up, young lady,' was his medical opinion. 'What are you doing in this town, anyway? How did you get here?'

'I might ask you the same, Doc,' Kelly smiled, as he poured her out a cup of coffee. She hesitated about telling Doctor Reynolds the whole story as she had been warned by Jim

Tobin that if the doctor had too much to drink, which was the reason why he had been struck off the medical register, he could easily say something about her and Jim which might get back to the law. Now that she had learned that they both were no longer being hunted, she did not want any lawman to reconsider the telegram he had received, and not especially since she had just spoken to the local sheriff who, Kelly had been quick to notice, had taken quite a shine to her.

Kelly realized, however, that there was not much else she could do, and hoped he could be trusted as she began her story. After a while Kelly finished speaking and took the last remaining mouthful of her coffee.

'You're riding with Jim Tobin?' Reynolds said with surprise. 'Please be careful, Kelly. When he has a few drinks he can turn nasty. I'd hate anything bad to happen to you.'

Kelly threw back her head and

exclaimed. 'Bad, Doc? I reckon I've had just about everything bad thrown at me by one man or another. I know what drink can do to men. Denver Branch was worse than usual to me when he'd had a few drinks. The gang in Larkinton had some good sport after a few drinks — remember the fight with Sandy Kaye? And Hay Bassett was a bit rough with me when he had me in Larkinton. Yeah, Doc, I know about men and drink. It can do bad things to men and they then do bad things to women and themselves.'

Reynolds looked thoughtful. This young woman before him certainly had guts and he admired her spirit that had obviously not been broken, despite everything.

'What I'm going to say to you now, Kelly, I'm not saying because I want your sympathy.'

Kelly looked a bit startled. 'What is it, Doc?' Kelly asked in concern.

'I haven't got long to live — a month at the most.'

Kelly's hand went straight to the doctor's. 'I'm real sorry to hear that.'

He shook his head dismissively. 'I've had my time, Kelly. We've all got to go at sometime or other. I'm not fretting about it. No, what I'm telling you for is this: I've stashed away quite a bit of money and I've no one to leave it to. Someone who deserves it should get it, and that someone is you. I'll leave myself with enough to see me through until the end.'

Kelly took the old man's other hand and squeezed them both. She didn't know what else to do.

'But you hardly know me, Doctor Reynolds. Why me? Isn't there anyone else you know better?'

'Oh I daresay there are others I've known for longer, young lady, but you are the most deserving. The money should see you through most of your life, if used sparingly of course.'

Kelly shook her head in utter desbelief. 'I can't take your money, Doc, it wouldn't feel right somehow.'

176

'It's what I want,' he said emphatically. 'No more arguments. I'd hate to think that Jim Tobin got the lot and ran out on you though. Are you sure he's the right man for you?'

'I feel sure he is. He's treated me really well while riding together.'

Reynolds' lips pursed into a thin line. 'Has he taken advantage of you at all while you've been together?' He didn't wait for her reply. 'You'll have to be rather careful now you're pregnant, Kelly. It could injure the baby — or you might even lose it.'

'I'm his woman now, Doc. He's been real gentle with me. I'm sure he really loves me — and I love him.'

Kelly got up to leave, still holding the doctor's hands.

'How did you get your money out of Larkinton when the posse took over the town and burned it to the ground?' Kelly was intrigued.

'When I was released without charge — I hadn't committed any crimes and had been a virtual prisoner, just like you — I went back to Larkinton and dug it up. I didn't want the gophers having it for a nest now, did I?' he smiled.

'Jim and I have considered going back to live in Paradise. It's good up there — just like I think the real Paradise would look like.'

Reynolds picked up an oblong parcel tied up with brown paper and string and handed it to Kelly.

'It sounds like quite a good idea. It'll be a bit lonely though. But if you're with the right man — and I sincerely hope Tobin is — then you'll be fine.'

Kelly went up on tiptoe and kissed the grey-haired, bewhiskered man on the cheek.

'I appreciate this, Doc,' she said, referring to the parcel. 'I really do. I'll come and see you again.'

Reynolds shook his head. 'Better not. We don't want the law to make links between us and come up with who you really are. By the way, you look charming in a dress, my dear. Take care of yourself — and be happy.' He walked her to the door. 'Goodbye, Kelly, and good luck.'

'Goodbye, Doctor Reynolds. And thanks.'

Jim Tobin had waited on the corner in the shadows while Kelly was inside. She had been gone about three-quarters of an hour but the wait seemed much longer. He decided to let her get to the hotel before him and see if she lied to him when he returned. He could see she was carrying a parcel. What on earth had she got there? he wondered.

Kelly unlocked the door to their room and crossed to the dresser and lit the lamp. Within five minutes Jim Tobin knocked on their door and she opened it to him. She could smell the liquor on his breath and it reminded her of when Hay Bassett had returned to her after locking her in the hotel room in Larkinton.

'You've been quite a while,' Kelly remarked.

'I wouldn't have thought you'da

noticed,' he said, 'you haven't been here yourself. I told you not to go visiting Doc Reynolds!' His voice was harsh and his face was as black as thunder. Kelly didn't like it.

'What did you say to the law? I saw you talking to the sheriff in the street.'

'He rescued me from the attentions of a drunk,' she explained. 'It's a good job I did speak to him. He thought he'd recognized me from a Wanted poster, but then said it couldn't possibly have been me as the woman died with another prisoner — Tobin — in a ravine, and that a US marshal had shot Hankins.' Kelly's face was open and smiling. She obviously hadn't tried to lie to him that she had never left the room.

Tobin began to feel ashamed that he could ever doubt her. He owed so much to this woman. He owed her his life.

'What yer got there?' he asked, pointing to the parcel she had dropped casually onto the bed.

'A legacy,' Kelly grinned up at him.

'What d'yer mean?'

'Poor old Doc Reynolds has about a month to live. He gave me his life savings because he said I deserved it. He said I'd got guts.'

Tobin frowned. 'A man don't just hand over all his money just like that,' he told her. 'What did you have to do for it?'

Kelly was stunned. She wasn't quite sure what he was implying, but began to get a good idea.

'What are you saying, Jim?'

'You know what I'm saying. Did he make you pay for all that money?'

Kelly's eyes flashed with fire and her hand gave Tobin a stinging blow across his face.

'How dare you?' she screamed at him. 'You're calling me a . . . a whore — someone who'd do it for money!'

Kelly felt heartbroken that Jim could possibly even think she'd do such a thing. Shooting two guards who had tried to rape her was one thing, but doing that — for money. She flung

181

herself on to the bed and sobbed quietly.

Jim lay down on the bed and drew her shaking body to him. He knew he had hurt her badly with such an insinuation and regretted it. It must have been the drink that had made him think such a thing about the woman he loved. He had punched Hankins for saying such a thing about her, yet here he was insinuating the same thing. He made a mental note to leave alcohol alone as it seemed to bring out the worst in him. He vowed there and then that he would never, ever, say or do anything to hurt this wonderful woman again. Doc Reynolds had been right: she had got guts. More than enough for both of them.

17

That night Kelly did not come to him as usual. She turned her back on him and only turned over in her sleep. Jim did not attempt to touch her at all as he felt his advances would be unwelcome at the moment. Perhaps by morning she would have forgotten about what he'd said to her and, hopefully, by then, would have forgiven him.

Jim was up and dressed by the time Kelly awoke. He was sitting in a chair watching her. Her heart dropped at the crestfallen expression on his face and she gave him a smile.

'Have you forgiven me for last night?' he asked her hopefully, and crossed the room and sat on the edge of the bed, taking her hands in his.

'Yes,' she replied. 'I think it must have been the drink that changed you, Jim. Maybe if you . . . left the drink alone?' she asked him carefully.

'I'd already decided that last night,' he said. 'I'm real sorry, Kelly. I don't know what's wrong with me. I just can't bear to think of any other man even touching you.'

'There's no need to be jealous, Jim,' she told him quietly. 'I'm your woman now, and I'd like it to stay that way, so long as you trust me — always — because you can, you know.'

He drew her to him and smothered her face with gentle kisses.

'You have my word,' he declared.

While at breakfast a thought flashed through Kelly's mind.

'Jim, that sheriff I spoke to last night. He said I looked like the picture on the Wanted poster. If he sees you with me, he'll recognize you, too. It would be more than a coincidence for two people together who looked like the pictures.'

'What shall we do then, leave town today?' he suggested. 'I had hoped you'd be able to rest up a bit before we travelled again.'

'I know. I asked him if he knew of employment in town and he suggested I ask here at the hotel. What if he comes checking up on how I got on?'

Jim looked worried. Things looked good for them when Kelly said that the law was no longer looking for them, but she was right. Seeing them both together would set the sheriff's mind working and wondering about them.

'I think we'd better pay the bill and leave,' said Jim at last. 'We've got a bit of cash now so we can restock our supplies.'

'I'd like to buy some more riding clothes. The ones I've got were not even my own!' she pointed out. 'They must stink a bit by now.' She smiled slightly.

'We'll shop separately,' Jim suggested. 'We'll pretend we don't know each other outside this hotel. It would be safest, I reckon.'

Kelly agreed. They went to their room and Kelly took some of the money from the wad of banknotes that

Doc Reynolds had given her and handed some to Jim.

'Get enough for us to carry easily,' she told him. 'We can always restock as we reach other towns.'

He nodded. 'But which direction have we decided we're going? Wyoming or Paradise?'

'Let's toss for it,' she suggested. 'Heads, Wyoming, tails, Paradise.'

Jim flipped a dollar coin and held his hand over it for a second, to keep Kelly guessing. He showed her his palm. The coin showed tails.

'Paradise it is then,' said Kelly. 'I'll leave the hotel first and you follow after five minutes,' she suggested.

While Kelly was gone, Jim Tobin counted out the money from the brown-paper parcel. It came to $20,000. Tobin gave a low whistle and tied the parcel up again and stashed it away in Kelly's saddle-bags.

Kelly found an outfitter's shop. One half of it was for gents' apparel and the other half stocked women's clothes.

Kelly needed some of each, especially new drawers. After purchasing these she went through a door and entered the gents' section and picked out some Levis, and two shirts. She had already got a hat that Jim had bought her in another town. The clothes were black, like the ones she picked out in Larkinton where she had been served by the Swede, Johann Larsen. She wondered what had happened to him. Had he perished in the fire in Larkinton, or had he been set free like Doc Reynolds? she wondered.

The middle-aged assistant gave her a strange look as he wrapped the garments.

'Going riding, Miss?' he asked her.

Kelly merely gave him a smile, paid for the goods, and left the store.

As she stepped outside she nearly bumped straight into the sheriff.

'Morning, miss,' he said cheerfully. 'Been shopping?' he nodded at the parcels.

'Yes, just a few things I needed,' said

Kelly cheerfully, although her heart-beats were beginning to quicken at the surprise of seeing the sheriff again so soon.

'Have you found yourself a job?' he asked her. 'I could put in a good word for you if you like?' he suggested.

'You're very kind, Sheriff, but you don't know me,' Kelly pointed out.

'Oh, I'm good at judging a character by their face. Now your face is an honest face, I'd bet my boots on it.'

Kelly gave him a beaming smile. 'That's very nice to know, Sheriff. Thank you! I'll ask around and give your name as a reference. Goodbye.'

He touched his hat to her and carried on walking along the street. Jim had just stepped out of the general store at that moment and he noticed the sheriff moving away from Kelly. How glad he was that they were not seen together. Jim gave a low whistle in relief.

Kelly went into the hotel and was soon followed by Jim.

'What was the sheriff saying to you?'

he asked when they'd both reached their room again.

'Just general pleasantries. He offered to give his name as a reference if I found myself a job. He said my face was an honest one and that he was good at judging characters.'

'Well you would have been honest if Hay Bassett hadn't started you on your life of crime,' Jim pointed out.

They sorted out their purchases and got them together to take to their horses. Kelly was dressed for riding and as she pulled down her hat further over her eyes, she could have been mistaken for a young man. She went on ahead while Jim checked out at the reception desk.

After paying the livery-man, they saddled up and secured their supplies on the horses.

'We could do with a wagon,' Kelly remarked. 'It wouldn't be so hard on the horses, carrying this lot.'

'Yeah, a good idea,' Jim agreed. 'We could mebbe sleep in it, too.'

'Perhaps we can pick one up at the next town?'

Jim nodded. He looked across at Kelly in her new riding gear, plus her gun on her hip. He smiled as he recalled how she had said that she felt naked without one. He was well aware that she was much faster with a gun than he was. He smiled to himself again as he knew full well that she was more than a match for any man. In fact he felt safer under her protection than he had with the whole Bassett gang.

Although the night before hadn't been their happiest spent together, at least sleeping in a bed had helped Kelly recover from the journey before. Jim felt more relaxed now that the Wanted posters on them had been taken down and unless they were recognized by a sharp-eyed lawman with a good memory, they would be comparatively safe. At least now they could rest up at a town without too much worry.

Jim Tobin was glad that he and Kelly

were back on friendly terms again. He had hated what had happened the night before. Although they had shared the same bed, they had been as far apart as if an iceberg had drifted in between them.

The money Doc Reynolds had given Kelly was the best medicine he could have prescribed. Now they could restock their supplies without having to worry about how to pay for them.

Jim no longer worried that the journey back was slow at times for they were not being hunted now and could stop whenever they felt the need. It was also much better without Hankins needling them all the time.

When they made camp for the night, Kelly snuggled up to Jim but she no longer wanted him to make love to her completely, as before. She had told him that Doctor Reynolds had suggested that it was not such a good idea bearing in mind the baby within her. Jim himself realized this and although he missed the complete closeness, he was happy enough to hold her and kiss her as before.

'Kelly,' he said that night, as they lay together, fully clothed, 'shall we get married at the next town?'

Kelly was quiet for a while as the suggestion sank in.

'Would I be Mrs Tobin, or would we have to choose another name do you think?' she asked.

'Then you agree that you'll marry me?'

'Of course!' she answered. 'We can afford a wedding ring now — thanks to Doc Reynolds.'

'Think of a good name to be married by then,' Jim told her. 'Let me know in the morning. Goodnight, Kelly.' He pulled the blankets higher up over his ears and shut his eyes.

'That's not fair!' Kelly exclaimed. 'You go leaving me with all the thinking to do while you go off to sleep!' She gave him a playful punch on his arm.

Jim laughed. 'You talk to much,

woman. Go to sleep and think in the morning.'

It was nice to hear Kelly giggle next to him. Everything seemed right with their world at that moment.

18

The next morning after breakfast Jim asked Kelly what name she had decided they would be called when they got married.

'I've thought it over, Jim, and I reckon that if we used a false name, then it wouldn't be legal.'

He agreed. 'Yeah, but it might be a bit risky using our real names.'

'Jim, I've never been inside a church before and I don't know which religion I am anyhow. Where would we get a wedding ring from? I've never seen no jewellers in any of the towns we've been in, and I don't reckon they'd sell them at a general store.'

Jim was thoughtful. He couldn't remember where he'd gotten the ring he'd given his wife.

'Can I ask you something?' Kelly began tentatively.

'What about?'

'Hay told me once that you shot your wife and her lover. Do you ever think about her?'

Jim got up from the ground and tipped the remainder of the coffee over the camp-fire and started picking up his bedroll.

'Sorry, Jim, it's none of my business,' said Kelly hastily. He stood before her, a certain sadness in his eyes as he replied, 'I reckon it is your business; after all, you intend to be my wife.' His breath became heavy before he continued.

'Marcy and me hadn't been married long — just over a year it was. I loved her and trusted her. I went into town about fifty miles away to buy some supplies and said I'd stay over for the night and return the day after. I didn't like the thought of her being in the house on her own so I decided to come back in the dark. It was a rough night and was raining hard and tumbleweeds were rolling around.

'I guess they didn't hear the buckboard through all that wind and I came in quiet like so I didn't disturb her. I lit a lantern and took it with me to our room. I had no idea what I'd see when I opened the door. There were the two of them in our bed together. I knew the feller — in fact I thought he was my friend. I just saw red, Kelly. I just . . . shot them both where they lay . . . in our bed.'

He was looking at the ground and Kelly got up and hurried towards him. Her arms went around him and she held him tightly against her.

'My poor Jim,' she said quietly. 'My poor, poor Jim. It must have almost destroyed you.'

He dropped the bedroll and the coffee pot he was holding and put his arms around her and stroked her hair. He felt almost relief at having told her.

'I know I have a jealous streak in me, Kelly. I can never bear to think of anyone else even touching you. I guess it all stems from that day.'

'Oh, Jim,' she breathed. 'I understand, I really do. You must trust me though. I'll never — ever — give you any cause to doubt me.'

He held her even tighter, so tight she could hardly breathe.

'I know, Kelly. I do trust you. I know that I can trust you with my life.'

'Come on, let's pack up camp,' she smiled up at him.

They mounted their horses and set off once more. Kelly's mind was still on the scene Jim had just painted. Since she had known him in Larkinton and Paradise, Jim Tobin had always been quiet and never smiled. She now knew why. What he had discovered that dark, stormy night, must have gnawed at him inside like a cancer. She decided she would never mention it again.

'Jim,' she began a little hesitantly, 'as both of us aren't religious, and we don't want to use false names, what if we had our own wedding ceremony — just you and me. We could say our vows to each other. That would be just as good as some preacher saying words over us. It would mean just as much to us, wouldn't it?'

He turned and looked at her pretty little face.

'If that's what you want, Kelly. It's fine by me.'

'Right,' she said, 'we'll do it around noon when we stop for a break. You'll have to say the words first as you know them.'

He shrugged his shoulders and thought for a moment.

'I can't remember all of them.'

'Never mind, just as long as we mean what we say, what does it matter if they're not all correct?' She looked to see his reaction, but as usual, his face was inscrutable.

They rode along in not too much of a hurry. Jim had an uncanny feeling they were being followed. He wasn't sure if Kelly was aware of it or not as she hadn't said anything. He guessed that being an outlaw for so long gave him a sixth sense about danger which served him in good stead over the years.

The sun was directly above them which was their clock that told them it was noon.

As Jim dismounted he looked all around him. There were riders in the distance, coming their way. They could be quite harmless, he realized, just travellers like themselves. On the other hand, they could be the law who had not received notification that all three of the fugitives were now dead, officially.

After they had eaten and taken a drink from their water canteens the two stood side by side.

'No ring!' Kelly reminded Jim.

He grimaced and pulled up a tuft of grass and twisted it together, then wrapped it round her ring finger.

'With this ring I thee wed, and with my body I thee worship and . . . ' he thought for a moment, 'and all my worldly goods I thee endow.' He looked into her eyes. 'Trouble is, I haven't got no worldly goods.'

Kelly laughed. 'Never mind, I'll settle for the first two.'

'Now you've got to say that you love, honour and obey me, till death do us part,' Jim told her.

'Well, I'll love you, Jim Tobin, and I'll honour you, but I won't obey you — *all* the time!'

He gave her a gentle smack on her bottom. 'You'd better had, young woman. I'm your husband now and you'll do as I say.'

'Well, I'm your wife, and I *might* obey you — sometimes.'

Jim shook his head in mock despair. 'I can see I'll have to take you over my knee and spank you hard, Mrs Kelly Tobin.'

'I'd like to see you try, Mr Jim Tobin!' She ducked away from him and he started chasing her until they both fell on the ground laughing.

Jim wrapped his arms around her and kissed her hard on her mouth and Kelly's eyes shut in ecstasy. She reckoned that was the best wedding anyone had ever had.

As night drew on they stopped to camp for the night in among a stand of trees. Jim had looked around him before they dismounted but had not noticed any riders in the vicinity. Maybe they had moved off in a different direction — he hoped.

They found some kindling for a fire and soon had the coffee pot on to boil. Jim got out the skillet and cut some strips off some salted pork and tossed in some beans to go with it. He was pleased to see that Kelly ate something for a change and guessed she must have felt hungry. Her constant sickness had seemed to have been less over the last few days and he hoped by now that she would be feeling a lot better in herself.

As they ate, Jim's ears were alert for the slightest snap of a twig or the sound of approaching horses or men's footsteps. He had no intention of them being caught unawares by bushwhackers, be they the law or outlaws.

'Kelly, I want you to be on the alert

tonight,' he warned. 'I saw two riders in the distance today. I haven't seen them the last two or three hours, but that don't mean to say that they aren't still around. Keep your gun inside your bedroll and be ready for any intruders.'

'OK, Jim,' said Kelly. 'I hope they don't shoot us while we sleep. Maybe we hadn't better sleep at all?'

'We could take it in turns,' Jim suggested.

'Good idea. You go first and I'll wake you in two hours — or when I think it's two hours,' she added.

They finished up their meal and cleared away the dishes. It was then that they heard horses approaching the camp.

'Howdy,' the first rider called before reaching them. 'Mind if we share your camp-fire tonight?'

The other rider drew up with the first. Both looked as if they hadn't washed or shaved for many months. It was difficult to see their faces beneath their beards and moustaches; it was practically dark also.

'We've just finished supper,' said Jim, 'but there's coffee still in the pot.'

'Thanks, much obliged,' said the first rider. The second, as yet, had not uttered a word.

'You're not the law, are you?' asked Kelly.

The first rider squinted at Kelly as he tried to see her face properly beneath her hat.

'Are you a woman?' he asked.

'I was when I last looked,' Kelly smiled, trying to sound confident, although she really felt afraid of these two before her.

'I asked you a question,' said Kelly.

The first rider shook his head. 'No we're not the law. Would it bother you some if we were?' he asked her.

'Well, let's just say that we wouldn't be all that happy about it. On the other hand, we wouldn't be all that happy if you aimed to kill us.'

Jim wished Kelly would shut up. These men might get irritated at a woman constantly talking and do something to stop her.

The men dismounted and tied their horses near the other two.

'We'd sure like a cup of that coffee, ma'am,' said the first man. 'Good of you to offer.'

Jim added some more kindling to the fire and the sparks flew up into the air, illuminating the two men's faces as they sat on their haunches and used the cups Kelly and Jim had already used.

'We'll bunk down here, if we may?' the first man asked, but did so before he received an answer. The silent one did likewise.

'I'm going to the privy,' Kelly whispered to Jim. 'Don't let either of them follow me. You know what happens to men who follow me to the privy, don't you?'

Jim knew only too well. The two guards on the prison wagon paid with their lives.

When Kelly returned to the camp-fire the two strangers appeared to be asleep. They were both snoring loudly anyway. At least they knew that if they stopped snoring, then that was the time to start worrying. Kelly intended staying awake for two hours as they had arranged before the men had actually arrived in camp, and then let Jim do his turn.

It was strange, Kelly thought to herself, that if you really wanted to stay awake, your brain told you to go to sleep. If she had wanted to go to sleep, then she knew she would not be able to.

At last the snoring stopped, which was the only sound that had been keeping Kelly awake. It ought to have alerted her that the two men were awake, but sleep claimed her.

Jim wondered if Kelly had stayed awake for the first two hours as they had agreed. She seemed still enough as if she had gone to sleep so he decided to stay awake himself.

When the two men ceased snoring, Jim's senses became heightened. The one who had done all the talking so far left his bedroll and moved away a few yards. It was only to relieve himself and he was soon back beneath his blankets. The silent one did likewise and Jim relaxed slightly. They seemed harmless enough. Maybe he and Kelly were too suspicious.

When Jim and Kelly awoke the next morning, their first thoughts were of the whereabouts of their two visitors. The men were still there, the one who talked was adding kindling to the fire which he had obviously relit.

''Mornin', ma'am, mister,' said the man. Kelly and Jim nodded and pulled back the blankets and stood up.

'Mind if we join yer for breakfast?' the talking one said.

'OK,' Jim agreed, but he would have preferred if the two had left before morning came.

Kelly started the coffee pot boiling and mixed some oats with water and sat the pan beside the coffee pot on the fire. 'Haven't you got your own mugs and dishes?' Kelly asked them, suspicion showing in her voice.

' 'Fraid not. Guess we'll have to share yours,' he said. Kelly flashed him a black look. This man was assuming too much for her liking, taking their hospitality for granted.

'Mebbe we could ride together?' He looked from Kelly to Jim.

'Sorry, but we like to ride alone,' came Jim's reply. 'Anyhow, why are you two so light with provisions and utensils?'

'We're kinda strapped for cash, you understand?'

'So are we,' Jim lied. He had no intention of letting these men know about Kelly's legacy from Doc Reynolds. 'We can't provide for two more.'

'Fair enough,' said the man. 'Sorry I suggested it. We've bin laid off from our job on a ranch west of here. We're looking for work elsewhere. Times are hard for cowboys lately.'

Kelly nodded. 'Times are hard for most folk, I reckon. It makes some folk turn to crime to get a crust.'

'You're so right, ma'am. Not many folk would be quite so understanding.'

Kelly and Jim ate and drank first, then let the other two use their mugs and dishes.

'Does your friend there, speak at all?' Kelly asked the other man.

'Billy-Bob likes fer me to do all the talking. Saves him having to think of the words to use,' he replied.

'What do we call you, ma'am, mister?' he asked.

'Call us what you like,' said Jim. He had no intention of giving them their real names. He still did not trust the two.

'Mr and Mrs What You Like,' he grinned. 'You two are married, ain't yer?'

'Most definitely,' Kelly interposed. 'Trouble is, we hadn't enough money for a ring. Sad that, ain't it?' She smiled slightly.

'I notice you wear a gun, ma'am. Is it for use or ornament?' he asked her.

'Put it like this,' Kelly replied, 'if I were you, I wouldn't try finding out.'

'Huh!' he exclaimed. 'I've never seen no woman good with a gun before.'

'As I just said,' Kelly gave another warning, 'don't do anything that would make me use it on you.'

By the man's expression, Kelly was aware that he did not believe her, but both let it go.

The men did not seem in any hurry to leave after breakfast and Kelly and Jim were becoming slightly uneasy. After they'd cleared away, they packed up their bedrolls and breakfast things, and saddled the horses and packed on their provisions.

'How about letting us have some of your supplies?' the talking man said.

Kelly and Jim exchanged glances.

'I could always take them,' he said, drawing his gun.

'You could at that,' said Kelly. 'Try saying that without a gun in your hand. Go on, I'm calling you out.'

The man threw back his head and

laughed. 'I wouldn't want to embarrass you, ma'am. Why not let your man here fight your battles for you?'

'I'm willing,' said Jim. 'It's the only way we're gonna finish this.'

Kelly put herself between Jim and the man holding the gun.

'It's me or no one. I call you, mister. Reholster your gun and stand back a pace or two.'

The four were silent for a few moments, each pondering over the events to come.

'If I were you, I'd get on your horses and get outa here now!' Kelly warned. 'It'd be a real shame if Billy-Bob here didn't have no one to speak up for him any more.'

'Oh well, ma'am, if it will make you happy, I accept your challenge. Pity though, your man here'll miss you I bet.'

'Kelly, forget it!' Jim told her. 'Give 'em some supplies and let's go.'

'Wise thinking, feller,' said the man.

'Reholster your gun, mister, and the

rest of you, stand back!' Kelly ordered.

Jim felt belittled by Kelly's actions. It should have been him facing the man instead of Kelly. It made him feel less of a man and it dented his pride. He realized now why Steve Culley had left her after he had watched her kill Hankins and wound the marshal.

'Are you ready?' the man asked her.

'Ready,' Kelly confirmed. She watched the man's eyes, as Hay Bassett had taught her. She stood loosely, almost nonchalantly, and this had the desired effect on the man. She looked too damned confident. Was he doing the right thing after all? he wondered. He did not have long to wonder. He decided to make the first move, but it wasn't fast enough. Kelly's hand drew, cocked and fired her gun before his gun even left its holster. The surprised expression on the man's face as he fell forward would remain in the onlookers' memory for some time to come.

'Sorry about that, Billy-Bob,' said Kelly as she reholstered her gun. She felt almost sorry for the man who had now lost his only friend, companion and tongue. Kelly felt in the pocket of her shirt where she had previously put a five-dollar bill. She crossed to the pathetic looking man and pushed the money into his shirt pocket and then mounted up.

'So long,' Kelly called over her shoulder. Jim just nodded. It had to happen, Jim was well aware of this fact. But somehow it didn't sit well with him.

He nudged his mount to catch up with Kelly who seemed in a hurry to leave the scene of death. Jim wondered how many more bodies they would leave behind before they reached Paradise.

19

After a few silent minutes had passed, Jim said, 'Pity that had to happen back there, Kelly.'

'I know,' she said a little wistfully. 'It's poor ol' Billy-Bob I feel sorry for. I doubt he can take care of himself without the talking one.'

'What was it you slipped into his pocket?' Jim asked.

'Five dollars. It's all I had on me without going to the bedroll.'

Jim allowed a slight smile to cross his lips. 'Oh, so you took it out of the saddle-bags?'

'Yeah,' she replied, 'I thought it would be safer with me. I guess I would've been proved right if I'd let him take what he wanted back there.'

Jim was silent for a while but Kelly knew what was on his mind.

'You thought it was your place to face

him, Jim, didn't you?' She watched his face for an answer, which he gave her after a pause.

'You made me look less of a man back there, Kelly. I wish you'd let me take care of things in future. I don't wanna keep having to hide behind your skirts all my life.'

Kelly gave a short laugh. 'But I don't wear skirts that often, Jim, or hadn't you noticed?'

Tobin's lips were pressed into a firm line. 'You know what I mean. I want to be the one in charge from now on, understand?'

'Yes, Jim, I understand,' she answered meekly, but Jim Tobin was well aware that she didn't mean it. During their wedding ceremony she hadn't promised to obey him, only when it suited her.

The journey was tiring and uneventful. They bypassed the town of Colfax as it was too near to where they had held up the stagecoach. Kelly had forgotten that incident temporarily and realized they could still be wanted for that job in the area. Their supplies were running out and Jim was becoming slightly worried. He had no idea when they'd reach another town where they could restock and rest up. The journey did not seem to be quite so hard on Kelly on their way back as it had on their way to Wyoming. Even now, Jim wondered if they were doing the right thing after all. What if Paradise had been taken over by others? Would there be another shoot-out to regain the place for themselves?

It was while they were filling their canteens at a creek that they were approached by two riders.

'Keep quiet and let me do the talking!' Jim ordered her. 'Don't let them see too much of your face.'

Kelly pulled her hat down further so the shade would cover her eyes.

'Howdy,' said the tallest of the two riders.

Jim nodded in acknowledgement. He noticed the two men were looking harder at Kelly than himself.

'Is there a town anywhere near here?' Jim asked them.

'About ten miles straight on, mister.'

Jim nodded his thanks and hung his now full canteen on to the horn of his saddle. Kelly did likewise and avoided eye contact with the men.

Jim looked back as they mounted up and noticed that the men were discussing them. One of the riders jerked his thumb in their direction, obviously wondering if Kelly was male or female.

'When we get up to Paradise, Kelly, you'll wear a dress all the time. I want to live with a woman in future. I've seen you in men's pants for long enough,' Jim declared with finality.

Kelly gave one of her cheeky smiles. 'Just as you say, Jim. You give the orders from now on.'

'Just you wait until I get you in that town's hotel bedroom, young woman. I'll teach you how a wife should behave to her husband.'

'Jim — I just can't wait!' she laughed,

and urged her mount into a gallop, forcing him to ride hard to catch her up.

The town was smaller than the other two they had been in previously and the hotel only had a few rooms. Luckily one of them was vacant when they went in to book it. The place was rather dingy but it was one that they would remember the most. In Colfax Jim had only lain with Kelly for an hour, fearing to free his emotions. In Brewster they had quarrelled when he'd accused her of taking money for favours from Doc Reynolds, and they had been cold towards each other. But here, in the town of Tall Trees, they fully expressed their love for each other and everything was perfect.

They bought a wagon and supplies in the town the next morning and were soon heading off again towards the burnt-out town of Larkinton and two miles on from there, Paradise, their final destination.

Kelly recognised the shape of the rocks which were on either side of the only entrance in and out of the town. She recalled the night when she had escaped the Bassett gang by muffling her horse's hooves, and riding back to her old homestead. She also recalled being brought back again when Hay Bassett and his men had found her. When the Marshal, Luke Dalton, and the posse finally rescued her from Hay Bassett in Paradise, the shape of the rocks remained imprinted in her mind.

Everywhere looked desolate and grim as they drove the wagon through the street of Larkinton. Every building was flattened and black from the fire that had swept through the place. Kelly could remember where the various buildings had been — the saloon, the hotel, the restaurant, Johann Larsen's general store, but there was not a single structure standing now.

Two miles on they came to the

narrow ledge. They would have to leave the wagon and ride the horses in, then return for the supplies. Jim decided to look around the place first — just in case the cabin was already occupied.

When Kelly and Jim reached the other side of the narrow ledge and passed between the boulders on either side of the pathway, they immediately noticed smoke coming from the chimney in the cabin. Both exchanged looks of disbelief and disappointment. They had so hoped that this place would now be their own for the rest of their lives together.

'Stay here!' Jim ordered her. 'I'll go in first to see who's in there.'

Kelly dismounted and held the reins of Jim's and her own horse and watched as he made his way to the cabin, via the corral where he would not be in line with the window. His gun was in his hand as he crept silently towards the place that had once been the home of the Bassett gang.

Tobin reached the door which was

slightly ajar and kicked it gently with his foot. It swung open and Tobin waited for any response from within.

'Who's there?' a voice called out from inside the cabin.

'Come outside where I can see you!' Tobin ordered.

He heard a man's footsteps approaching the doorway and Tobin stood to one side. The man stepped outside the cabin and faced Tobin, a gun in his hand.

'Culley!' Tobin hissed out the name. 'What the hell are you doing here?'

'I could ask you the same,' Steve replied. 'Where's Kelly — is she with you?'

Jim Tobin pointed towards the two boulders and Steve Culley saw the woman he had left behind standing waiting with the horses. She was dressed in black, the same as he had found her here at this same cabin when he, Luke Dalton, and Joe Lilley had come to save her from Bassett — his own father. It was as if there had been a time-slip — that events over the past few weeks had never happened. But they had. Kelly had gone with Jim Tobin and Steve reckoned she was this man's woman now. He had had his chance and had thrown it all away.

Jim beckoned Kelly over, but dreaded Kelly's reaction when she saw the young man she had escaped the Bassett gang to find. Kelly had married him in their own fashion, but maybe that was only because she believed she would never see Culley again, after he had rejected her.

Kelly walked with the horses. At that distance she could not see who the man was standing in the doorway, but as she drew closer his features became clearer. Her heart seemed to lurch out of her chest at the sight of him. Steve. But he looked so much like his father, Hay Bassett. It was as if she was seeing Hay standing there like he had that day Denver Branch and the rest of the men had dragged her up to Paradise that first time, after she had received the beating from Sandy Kaye.

Jim Tobin watched Kelly's face carefully. What was she thinking? he wondered. How glad was she to see Culley again?

'Steve,' was her only response.

'Hello, Kelly. How are you?' he asked her.

'Fine. And you?'

He nodded. 'Fine. It's good to see you again. You and Tobin here are officially dead — did you know that?' he asked.

'Yes, I found that out.' She looked at Jim and although it was always hard to fathom out his inner feelings, she had the idea that he was both sad and angry that Steve Culley had crossed their path once more.

'What happens now?' Kelly asked the two men. 'Jim and I had hoped to live here from now on.'

Steve Culley sighed. 'It's a nice spot, here. I can't blame you for wanting to come back, in spite of all the memories, Kelly.'

Steve turned and ushered them into the cabin. 'There's coffee on the stove. Come on in.'

As Kelly entered the large one-roomed building, memories did come flashing back into Kelly's mind. Her own bed was by the door, where Hay had placed her after he had lifted her down from her horse. He had been so gentle and kind, she recalled. He had told his men what they could expect if any of them ever again laid a hand on her. They had all heeded his warning, but Hay had spent most days with her by the pool, teaching her how to draw and fire a gun, for her own protection.

'How long have you bin here?' Jim asked Steve.

'About a week.'

'How is Marshal Dalton? I hope I didn't damage his hand too much?' said Kelly.

'It'll never be quite the same again, I reckon, so he's gonna retire and marry Sarah Dobson.'

Kelly was sorry that she had been the

223

cause of him having to retire, but glad also that Sarah Dobson was to become a bride to the man she had wanted for so long.

They drank their coffee like old friends, but Jim was fully aware that they could never become real friends.

'Are you gonna move out, Culley?' Jim asked bluntly. ''Cos as sure as hell all three of us can't live here together.'

Steve looked at Kelly. She was still just as beautiful as he remembered.

'I guess not,' he replied. 'We could toss a coin for it, I suppose. Heads I leave, tails you leave.'

'And Kelly,' Jim added.

'No, just you,' Culley told him.

'You can stop that right now!' Kelly stood up, putting her coffee mug down on one of the bunks. 'No one gets me with a toss of a coin! I married Jim, Steve, so I stay with him, whether we stay here or leave. You already told me you didn't want me no more. There's no going back to how we were months ago.'

'Tobin, here, has already told me I was a fool to run out on you, Kelly. I agree with him, I was a fool. I still love you, you know.' His eyes had not left her face for quite a while, Tobin had noticed. 'So you got married, did you? I don't see no wedding ring.'

'We didn't need one. We did our own ceremony with our own words. It's just as good,' Kelly smiled up at Tobin.

'We should be together, Kelly,' Steve told her decisively. 'I've spent months of my life looking for you, and I can't let you go again, not now that I've found you once more.'

Jim Tobin was breathing heavily. He wanted to kill Steve Culley and get him out of their lives once and for all. While he was still around, Kelly would always be hankering after him, he was sure of that. He would always be at the back of her mind from now on.

'If you won't settle this with the toss of a coin, then we'll have to do something more drastic,' said Jim.

Culley looked him straight in the eye

and knew exactly what the man was getting at.

'We have a shoot-out?' he confirmed the as yet unvoiced suggestion.

'Exactly,' said Tobin.

'No!' Kelly broke in. 'I have a say in this. It's over me, anyhow. I love you both. I don't want either of you to die.'

'It's the only way, Kelly,' Jim told her. 'It'll never be over until . . . it's over,' he finished slowly. He jerked his head towards the door for Culley to follow him.

'No! No! I won't allow it!' Kelly yelled after them.

'Keep out of this, Kelly. Just for once, let me make the decisions,' Jim told her. 'Stay in the cabin until it's all over — one way or the other.'

20

The two men walked a few yards from the cabin and stood facing each other about twelve feet apart. Jim Tobin doubted his speed with a gun. Except for killing his wife and her lover in cold blood, he had not killed anyone else since he had belonged to the Bassett gang. He had left that for the others to do if it was necessary. He knew he would never have been able to out-draw Kelly and wondered how fast this young man would be.

Steve Culley was wondering the same as he stood there, arms slightly arched at his side. He had never used a gun except for once when he had killed his own father at almost the same spot as they were both standing now. He had practised the draw almost incessantly while he had rested up at an Apache camp. Steve had been made an honorary Apache after he had helped deliver the baby of an Apache squaw when she went into premature labour, and it was she who found him after Hankins and Quincey had broken most of his bones. He knew he was fast on the draw, but he was not at all sure about Tobin's speed. It was obvious that Kelly loved Jim Tobin and he knew they had been lovers during their flight from the law. Steve, on the other hand, had only ever had a brief kiss from her sweet lips. If he did kill Tobin, would she hate him for it? he wondered. Would she ever forgive him?

There was no more time for thinking. The moment had come, Steve saw it in the other man's eyes.

They drew in unison and a bullet made the final decision.

Kelly sat on the edge of the bed that had been hers while she lived with the Bassett gang. She twisted her fingers in her lap and felt sick inside. Which one of them would walk in that door? Which one of them did she want to walk in that door?

She loved Jim Tobin, enough to go through their own special wedding ceremony. But if Steve had not forsaken her after he and Marshal Dalton had come upon them on the trail, she would be with Steve now. Would they have been happy together? she wondered. Would she have loved Steve as she had loved Jim?

Such a lot had happened to her since she was dragged away from him by Denver Branch at their meeting place by the river. She knew she was an entirely different woman from that young, innocent girl he had fallen in love with. That was why he had forsaken her when they had met up again. Surely life together now would never work out?

Her thoughts were savagely broken into by the gunshot outside the cabin. Her heart seemed to turn over inside her breast and it felt as if it had stopped beating for a few moments before it started to race. It had happened. The deed had been done. It could not be reversed now.

She stood up and faced the closed door and began to tremble.

Time seemed to be ticking away so slowly for Kelly. Why didn't that door open? Why didn't she know how her life would continue and with whom?

At last the door opened slowly, very slowly, and Steve Culley stood before her, his face ashen.

Kelly was both glad and sorry at the same time. She pushed past Steve and ran towards the prone body of her lover. He lay on his back with his arms outstretched by his side as if on a cross. There was a large red bloodstain on his shirt covering his heart. Steve watched as she lay down beside the man he had just killed and put her arms around him. Her head was on Tobin's chest and Culley could see Kelly's body shaking with silent tears.

He left her alone with her grief and wondered how she would have reacted if Tobin had killed him.

It was an hour later before Kelly finally entered the cabin. Steve was lying on one of the bunks, his hands beneath his head. He looked across at her in the doorway and stood up immediately and came to her.

'I wish that hadn't happened, Kelly. I really do. I know how much you loved that man.' He placed his hands lightly on her shoulders and looked down at the tear-stained face upturned to his.

'It could as easily have been you lying out there, Steve. I would have been just as upset whichever one of you it had been.'

He held her close to his chest. 'If I hadn't turned up here you two might have been happy together. No doubt you had already forgotten me?'

'Not entirely,' she admitted. 'I reckon that was what Jim was worried about. He knew I'd never really get over you. You'd always be at the back of my mind somewhere.'

Steve stroked her hair which had now reached her shoulders. It would be nice

231

to see it again as he remembered it — long and shining brightly in the sunlight.

'Will we be OK together, Kelly?' Steve asked. 'I wish I hadn't rejected you back there on the trail. None of this would have happened then,' he said, indicating Jim Tobin lying outside.

'What is done, is done,' she said with finality. 'We must start life afresh from now on. There is something I must do,' she said, and left the cabin.

Steve Culley watched as she walked towards the two boulders leading to the narrow ledge. He frowned. What on earth was she going to do now? he wondered.

A while later Kelly returned. There was quite a transformation in her. Gone were the men's pants, shirt and hat. In their place Kelly was wearing a dress, and she was holding a brown-paper parcel tied up with string.

She entered the cabin once more and placed the parcel on the table.

'This is my legacy from Doc

Reynolds. I met up with him in one of the towns we called at. He said he'd only got a month at the most to live and wanted me to have his life savings. He'd got no one else to leave them to,' Kelly explained.

She noticed Steve admiring her in a dress once more, as he had seen her in Hazelworth.

'Jim said I'd got to wear a dress once we reached Paradise. Said I must be a woman from now on.' She lowered her eyes and continued, 'Pity he can't see me in it.'

Steve could not help but notice the catch in her voice. He knew it would take quite a while before she got over Jim Tobin, but he understood and was willing to wait until she was ready to belong to him again.

* * *

The next morning, down in the valley by the rock pool, Steve and Kelly stood at the graves of the two outlaws, Hay

Bassett and Jim Tobin. Both men had loved her and she had loved them in return. Now she stood beside Steve, her first and last love. Steve's arm rested lightly on her shoulder and they turned and walked back to the cabin which would be their home together.

THE END

We do hope that you have enjoyed reading this large print book.

Did you know that all of our titles are available for purchase?

We publish a wide range of high quality large print books including:
Romances, Mysteries, Classics
General Fiction
Non Fiction and Westerns

Special interest titles available in large print are:
The Little Oxford Dictionary
Music Book, Song Book
Hymn Book, Service Book

Also available from us courtesy of Oxford University Press:
Young Readers' Dictionary
(large print edition)
Young Readers' Thesaurus
(large print edition)

For further information or a free brochure, please contact us at:
Ulverscroft Large Print Books Ltd.,
The Green, Bradgate Road, Anstey,
Leicester, LE7 7FU, England.
Tel: (00 44) **0116 236 4325**
Fax: (00 44) **0116 234 0205**

Other titles in the
Linford Western Library:

STONE MOUNTAIN

Concho Bradley

The stage robbery had been accomplished by an old woman. Twine Fourch had never heard of a female being a highway robber before. He followed the trail all the way to a dilapidated log cabin up Stone Mountain. What happened after that no one could believe even after townsmen from Jefferson found the old log house and the skeletal dying old woman. But before the mystery could be solved there would be two unnecessary killings, a bizarre suicide and a lynching.

GUNS OF THE GAMBLER

M. Duggan

Destitute gambler Ben Crow arrives in Mallory keen to claim his inheritance, only to discover that rancher Edward Bacon has other ideas. Set up by Miss Dorothy, who had fooled him completely, Ben finds himself dangling on the end of a rope. Saved from death, Ben sets off in pursuit of Miss Dorothy, determined upon retribution. However, his quest for vengeance turns into a rescue mission when she is kidnapped by a crazy man-burning bandit.

SIDEWINDER

John Dyson

All Flynn wants is to be Marshal of Tucson, but he is framed by the territory's richest rancher, Frank Buchanan, and thrown into Yuma prison. Five years later Flynn comes out, intent on clearing his name and burning for vengeance. Fists thud, knives flash and bullets fly as he rides both sides of the law and participates in kidnapping and double-dealing. He is once again arrested for a murder of which he is innocent. Can he escape the noose a second time?

THE BLOODING OF JETHRO

Frank Fields

When Jethro Smith's family is murdered by outlaws, vengeance is the one thing on his mind. He meets the brother of one of the murderers, who attempts to exploit Jethro's grudge in the pursuit of his own vendetta. The local preacher, formerly a sheriff, teaches Jethro how to use a gun. With his new-found skills, Jethro and his somewhat unwelcome friend pit themselves against seemingly impossible odds. Whatever the outcome lead would surely fly.

SEVEN HELLS AND A SIXGUN

Jack Greer

Jim Cayman had been warned about Daphne Rankin, his boss's wife, and her little ways. When Daphne made a play for Jim and he resisted, the result was painful and about what he had feared. But suddenly matters went beyond the expected and he found himself left to die an awful death. Only then did he realise that there was far more than a woman scorned. He vowed that if he could escape from the hell-hole he would surely solve the mystery — and settle some scores.